Sue g … phone. He's … nly her temp… to the teleph… 'Hello? Misery Centre. Can I help you?'

She's all set to take down a message when the receiver is whipped from her grasp and she flinches, expecting a clout across the head. But the man who grabbed it simply gives her an exasperated look before assuming his oiliest voice to say down the receiver: 'Hello? Job Centre. I'm very sorry about that, we're having a bit of trouble with some of the youngsters . . .'

# SCORCHED EARTH

Edward Fenton

**A STAR BOOK**
*published by*
the Paperback Division of
W. H. ALLEN & Co. PLC

A Star Book
Published in 1985
by the Paperback Division of
W. H. Allen & Co. PLC
44 Hill Street, London W1X 8LB

First published in Great Britain by Sinclair Browne Ltd, 1984



Printed in Great Britain by
Hunt Barnard Printing Ltd, Aylesbury, Bucks.

ISBN 0 352 31610 1

# CONTENTS

# SCORCHED EARTH

# *Wednesday*

## *Looking for work*

Admiral Nelson – now didn't he have an affair with your Queen?

No sir, he had an affair with Lady Hamilton, who is buried in Highgate Cemetery. He once killed a polar bear with the butt of his musket. It was he who coined the immortal phrase – 'England expects'.

Chris flicks through his selection of postcards of London. 'Only 15 pence each. Postcards. Postcards? Picturesque views of the city?' It's not been such a bad day for postcards, a dozen sold already and it's only noon; but no one wants a guided tour. It's too cold, it's always too cold in this poxy place, and the wind blows most of his words away.

'Here on the left, London's oldest pub, the Duke of Clarence. The first Duke of Clarence drowned in a bowl of Marmite. He was a great gambler, and used to insist that his beer was served to him warm, so starting a custom which is universally observed in England today.'

A paunchy businessman looks alarmed to see him talking to himself. Chris whips out a map of London's underground and brandishes it saying, 'Tube maps, wonderful souvenirs? Only 20 pence!' But no, better stick to the real tourists. German couples are good but they know too much about English history. American couples are the star pick but the men get grumpy.

'Good afternoon! I'm a history student at London University. Would you like a guided tour?'

'I didn't come here for a good time!' a middle-aged man snaps back.

'Good afternoon! I'm a gliding student at St Mary's Penitentiary. Would you like a mystery tour?'

Office workers and civil servants are converging on the pub in groups of three or four swaggering men to every one simpering woman. The men are vying in loudness and grossness, while the women are trying to decide which of them is the least stupid.

A couple in matching tweed coats and hats are studying a copy of *What's Where*. 'You don't want to see any of the rubbish showing at the moment,' Chris tells them. 'I'd like to introduce you to some real English culture – only five quid for the pair of you.'

The man steps back and stares at Chris through his thick refracting lenses. 'If you lay a hand on my wife,' he says tremulously, 'I'll personally call your Police!'

Sod this, Chris thinks as he walks on, there must be easier ways of earning a few quid. He'd probably be more successful luring Japanese businessmen into the peep-shows of Soho – but no, no, that's not his scene at all. He does have morals you know, he'd never do anything to bring shame on his family; but for sure it's a sick world where culture and history are valued less than sin and fantasy.

No 10. 'And now on your right you can see Downing Street, the home of our Leader. Changing of the Guard takes place every hour. There was a time when the street was accessible to the general public, but now only close personal friends and television crews are allowed through the gates.'

A truckload of policemen trundles by, looking for trouble. Across the road a ruly party of Japanese tourists is staring at the House of Commons. Chris sees an opportunity for rich pickings, and tries to dodge through the traffic to reach them. But he gets stranded in the middle and watches helplessly as they're herded back into the seclusion of their coach.

A cold wind blows in from the river and bites his hands until they throb. His numb fingers suddenly preoccupy his whole being and make him forget his guidelines.

Now it begins to spit with rain. A flabby-faced boy dashes across Chris's path and attempts to convert a pigeon over the parapet of the House of Commons. The pigeon changes course midway and glides into a Gothic arch for shelter. Chris decides to find a shelter too, and rushes towards the main entrance.

'Oi! Members only!' hollers a uniformed man by the door.

'But it's raining,' Chris protests.

'What you got, then – a petition against it?'

'I'm looking for a job. Are there any vacancies here?'

'What kind of work d'you want?' the official asks, causing Chris's heart to miss a beat with anticipation. 'You think you could take over from Mrs Thatcher then?' and he bursts out laughing. Chris realises that he's being taken for a fool. Ha, ha, what's so funny then? Yes, if you want, I *will* take over from Mrs Thatcher. Thanks for the offer, I'm sure I'll be able to do much better than her. But the man goes on laughing. 'Here, Jim, come here!'

Chris turns and leaves, shaking with anger and shame. He'll not be treated like a dumb provincial. He looks around to see if there's any trade to solicit, but the pavement is suddenly deserted. Maybe it's a good thing – how would you ever explain British democracy to a foreigner, without starting a war about it?

He turns up the collar of his jacket and thrusts his hands deeper into his trouser pockets. His pockets ripped long ago through too much thrusting. When he forgets, his boots double up as his wallet.

The gardens by the river are beginning to look alive, but Chris decides not to drum up any trade there. He'd be taken for a drug-pusher for sure. Gleaming new cars rush past as he carries on down Millbank wondering where the hell he's going. A couple of elderly ladies look at him nervously and step out of the way.

Perhaps I'll go down to the Tate Gallery – it'll be warmer in there, and someone's bound to need a guide. I'll put on my glasses and look very studious! I'll be – a student at the Royal Academy of Art, trying to keep body and soul together on a meagre grant. Forty masterpieces in an hour, only four quid. Less than the price of a dirty tour round the city. I've got all the facts at my fingertips, they're just a bit frozen at the moment. Let's see now . . . strength of line – colour – pioneer of technique – son of a barber.

Crossing the road – watch out for the Rollses! The chauffeur's probably under orders not to brake for proles.

He decides to make a dash for it, and is about to fling his body forward, when there's a sharp blast on a horn to his left. A motorbike has broken through the stream of traffic and is haring towards him like a homing missile. He swings back his arms and manages (though it's touch-and-go at first) to keep his balance on the central reservation. He looks around to see if anyone's watching, and catches sight of the motorbike as it speeds off into the distance. Sorry, sorry about that!

Shit, he didn't see that at all. If it wasn't for that horn and his quick reflexes he'd've gone straight into the middle of the road and been swept away. What a close shave! Ended up pillioned on the handlebars.

Maybe, he thinks, wiping the shaken grin off his face, maybe the Lord *is* up there, looking after me, after all.

# *Am I invisible?*

Christ all fucking mighty, lucky that stupid wally wasn't driving a car – he'd've gone straight into me! People are like chickens, running into the road without looking. I mean, am I invisible or what?

You can't let your concentration slip for a moment. The parked cars are the worst, lying in wait ready to leap out at you at any second. Dan only feels safe when he's roaring ahead of the crowd, when he can see everything that's going on around him and doesn't have to worry about cars and people blindly bashing into him. He zips down one-way streets, over pavements, dodges traffic islands and shoots through red lights, all to avoid being choked and crushed and trampled by the traffic.

Passing the Houses of Parliament – woe betide anyone who cuts him up now, these pompous bastards in their flashy cars! It's not jealousy he feels for these people, it's contempt. What a burden, he thinks, to be called 'The Honourable' or 'Sir' or 'The Duke of'. It's like a man tattooing 'Aren't I beautiful' on his face, and then watching his face grow blotchy and wrinkled and haggard. Or it's like someone adopting the title of Saint – 'Well yes, of course, I am a messenger from the Almighty, I am elevated above all the rest of you.' Such conceit. Can you argue with conceit like that? Or can you only make it feel uncomfortable by deluging it with abuse and saliva?

Brought to a halt by a set of traffic lights, Dan leans disrespectfully against a parked Mercedes. There's a loud voice from a man in a car which has just pulled up beside him – 'How would you like somebody to scratch *your* car!'

Dan looks round and sees a blob of a middle-aged man dressed in a combat jacket and sitting in a shiny new land-rover. Two little boys, too young to know better, are sniggering on the back seat.

'I haven't got a car,' Dan shouts back crassly, deliberately misunderstanding. 'Mind your own business.'

'How would you like someone to scratch your car,' the man shouts again.

'D'you always stick your nose in other people's business?' Dan says. He's interested and disgusted by the combat jacket; he thinks the man must be an army officer, he has greasy hair, short all round but long at the top, pudding-bowl style.

'At least I'm civilised,' the man says, grinning, and making the boys split their sides with excitement, 'which is obviously more than you are!'

The lights turn green and Dan sees the chances of a full-scale argument slip away. He wants to talk about the army, about society and aggression. But there's no time. If the blobman wants a philistine, he'll play along with him. For a moment he wants his little bike to be a huge belching chopper, he wants to let off a huge stinking fart of black smoke. Toot! Toot!

'You fucking asshole,' Dan shouts out. 'You're a fucking nosey asshole.'

And the man, embarrassed that his sons might pick up this foul language, bursts out laughing in an attempt to drown out Dan's abuse. 'Ha! Ha! Ha!' he's saying, meaning to say, You're a philistine and I'm not, but actually saying, Don't listen to him boys, you mustn't hear what this savage is saying, you're never to learn words like that. Ha! Ha! Ha! you fucking – HAHAHAHAHA – asshole!

Dan roars off and escapes down a side-turning. And he's laughing heartily, too, at the blobman's clumsiness. Hahaha!

Heading north, up Regent Street, the traffic is thicker and even more erratic. The boss's wife has a lot to do today, she must buy some theatre tickets and look around the shops. She always has problems parking, but she must stop off for a capuccino, and amidst the tropical fronds of the coffee shop she can have a little personal crisis – lose something, maybe. 'Oh waiter, this is terrible, I've just lost some time!' 'How much, madam, and when did you last notice it slipping away?' They look for it under the table and outside the doorway and when at last they realise that it's gone for ever, she becomes fretful and dashes off to Old Bond Street to buy a necklace to calm her down.

Dan sees her walking down the street, he sees time slip through holes in her pockets, he lets it go to waste. He has other things to concentrate on – the left hand side of the road, still fine, the right hand side of the road . . . Sitting well forward, his bum almost directly above the engine, he fancies himself as a medieval jouster or a bringer of portentous news. He roars through a set of traffic lights as it's turning red, and then he's brought to a halt at the next set.

Down the street he sees a rich young woman dressed all in furs, leading a dog at the end of a 20-foot lead. She's taking it slow and easy so that everyone can stop and gawp at this lady of leisure; so smug, so proud, *she's* not going to risk stepping in any dog-shit, that's why she keeps the creature 20 feet away and no love goes down that line. Oh damn, now she wants to cross the road – the lights are about to turn green and the chihuahua is busy sniffing a lamp-post. But the lady is determined to cross, she extends the lead even further, and Dan revs his engine impatiently and toots his horn. The lady turns and gives him a dirty contemptuous stare and Dan wishes he had a pair of scissors, he'd like to grab the lead and cut it in two. The lady's wearing a slit skirt and her right thigh flashes as she walks.

Oh God, Dan thinks, I hope she doesn't think I tooted my horn because I could see her thigh. She probably thought I was leching over her. And he wonders if he should follow her and tell her, it's alright he wasn't leering at her, he was thinking what a hard face she has and so ugly and how dare she hold up the traffic. She wouldn't understand, though; *Roderick* thinks she looks gorgeous, especially in her fur jacket and slit skirt – 'Well it's such a lovely colour!'

The people look sadder as you leave the city centre. Dan gets caught behind a dumper-truck and has to lower his visor to protect him from the clouds of black smoke. You can feel the brain damage the fumes give you as you ride down the street. Some pedestrians still think the air is too clean, so they smoke cigarettes as they walk along to make sure they get a real lungful of poison and dirt. Every cigarette cuts your life by three minutes and down your high street there's a race to die, people puffing their way to a smelly grave and every time you yawn in a mouthful of London smog your IQ goes down a point.

In the opposite direction, towards the West End, there's a solid line of traffic. Suddenly a blue saloon car breaks ranks and lurches into Dan's path, blocking the road. The truck brakes violently, swerves, and mounts the pavement. Dan overtakes and manages to draw level with the car as it completes the turn.

'Brainless goons!' He glares at the occupants – two businessmen in suits. What if there'd been someone on the pavement back there? The businessmen look stony-faced as their car gathers speed – they obviously don't give a shit. They're probably too engrossed in their opera on the radio. Dan's blood boils. He puts the bike into third gear and reaches out and grabs the car aerial; then he releases the accelerator a little and the aerial comes away cleanly in his hand. He looks at his trophy for a second then flings it away, makes a sharp left turn and flees down a residential side-street.

He looks in his mirror nervously a few times before realising that he's not going to be chased. The a-hole knows he was in the wrong, driving like an Old English sheepdog – he's lucky he didn't kill someone.

Dan becomes even angrier when he realises what would've happened if the truck hadn't been at the head of the queue: the car would've ploughed straight into him instead. He reckons he's let them off lightly, he feels like going back and kicking the car to shit and ripping off the windscreen wipers as well. But he laughs when he remembers the men's faces. He tries to imagine the scene in slow motion: the look of horror and impotence on the driver's face, the futile dive for the automatic button to lower the aerial, and then – Dan's deft seizure of the booty and the moment of triumph as he brandishes it before hurling it away like the bit of rubbish it is.

One day, he vows, he'll rig up a paintstripping device to his handlebars, so that he can dole out real punishment to the cars which try to kill him. But he relaxes a bit as he nears home. It is my duty, he says to himself, to bring all the dozy reckless drivers to their senses; it is my duty to clear up the streets.

'I will not rest, nor will my engine grow cold, until the maniacs at the wheel have learnt to drive, or sold their cars, or taken a final plunge through the windscreen.'

## *What can you do?*

When Ratface wakes up he knows it's late. It always is. He stretches out his arm and turns on the radio beside his bed.

*The Government is considering a proposal to cut unemployment benefit this year. A spokesman has said that people on the dole must be prepared to tighten their belts.*

Tighten our belts! Shite, I pawned mine long ago! He turns the radio off but it's too late, he won't be able to get back to sleep again now. That really winds me up, that does – bloody Government. I need a smoke to calm me down.

He gets up and pulls on his jeans and a shirt. The flat seems very quiet. He rubs his eyes and wonders why his head feels so throbbing and dry. Too much of that bloody Lapsang Souchong tea last night, he knew it was going to dehydrate him! He staggers out of his room and down the narrow corridor. The whole flat is in shadow and gloom, so he gets a shock when he switches on the kitchen light and finds Sue, silently sipping a cup of tea in the corner.

'Sorry Sue, didn't see you there. You been up long?'

'No, not long.'

'Is there a cuppa tea going? Oh shit – it's a bit of a tip in here isn't it.'

'You can say that again!' She bangs her cup down onto the table. 'A bloody mess this room is, it's disgusting, I don't know how you can stand it. It's enough to make me want to throw up!'

'Well how come you've been sitting here all morning?'

'Where else am I going to sit? In my bedroom, just because of you? Mind you I might've been better off sitting in the dustbin, it's a lot cleaner than here!' She pushes away the ashtray which is overflowing with butt-ends and ash. 'How come you can't even get it together to empty an ashtray? Because you think the whole floor's one big bloody ashtray, don't you?'

Ratface looks at the floor and the kitchen rug and finds them strewn with ash and dead matches. There are also about a dozen cigarette ends standing on the table and the sideboard and the window-ledge, each with a neat stack of dead ash. Ratface tries to clear one of them away, and tips the ash all over the table.

'I was going to clear it all up, honestly,' he says. 'I was just too wasted last night . . .'

'Wasted! Wasted! I'll show you wasted! *I'll* fucking waste *you*! Who was here last night, eh? Who set fire to my Ronald Reagan candle?'

'Oh no . . .' He looks at the grotesque melted face. 'Oh shit, I forgot. I'm sorry, that was Tonio . . . I'm sorry, I'll buy you another one . . .'

'Yeah? In a year's time? That's how long it'll take you to save enough money.'

Ratface shakes his head. 'See, we ran out of matches, and Tonio said —'

'Pathetic excuse!' Sue exclaims. 'Ran out of matches . . . You just smoke too much dope, don't you. Too stoned all the time! You and your fucking dope . . .'

Now Ratface looks offended, as if someone's mortally insulted his best friend. 'Now, there's nothing wrong with dope! How'd you like it if you shared the flat with a couple of drinkers? Have a bunch of drunks round here every night, shouting and singing and smashing the place up?'

'Personally I'd like to share the flat with two nice tidy women. I've got no intention of moving in with any alcoholics.'

'At least we're quiet, aren't we? Did we keep you awake last night?'

'No, but I was so knackered nothing would've kept me awake.'

'A bunch of alcoholics would've kept you awake, I can tell you. Rowdy drunks. At least dope keeps you mellow.'

'Mellow! Mellow! Who wants to be mellow!' She puts on a whining American accent – ' "Oh we-ell, maan! Don't bother to empty the ashtrays, maan! We're just coming to terms with our environment!" How come you need mellowing out all the time, anyway? It's not as if you lead a very strenuous life.'

'Whaddaya mean, not very strenuous? Every Labour MP knows that life on the dole is a great strain. Unemployed people live shorter than people with jobs, that proves it must be a strain.'

'Or they smoke too much marijuana. The way you carry on, you're going to be senile at 40, I can just see it.'

'Oi! Give it a rest! Huh. Perhaps you'd prefer it if I did lots of speed instead. Then you'd have us desperately vacuuming the house at four in the morning.'

'Why d'you have to *do* –' Sue starts, but at this moment the front door slams shut. In comes Dan, helmet under his arm, his face glowing red from the cold outside.

'Jesus Christ – Hasn't anyone cleared this place up yet?'

'Isn't it foul,' says Sue. 'They didn't think of clearing it up last night – left me to sit in a disease-ridden pit all morning. My teacup had beer and fag-ends floating in it, 'sprobably contaminated now. Very nice that is for your morning cup of tea, "A Fine Blend of China Tea, Gnats-piss and Nicotine".'

Ratface sweeps some ash into his palm and sighs. 'Hey, you're back early, aren't you Dan? You taking a lunch break or something?'

'Ha! No.' Dan sits down. 'Got the sack, didn't I.'

'Eh? Just like that? No, you can't just get the sack, just like that.'

Dan smiles. 'All right then, they "gave me my notice". Same thing, isn't it. Told me they wouldn't be needing me after the end of the month. Bloody cheek. Expected me to sit around calmly till then and then just leave without a squeak.'

'So – what did you do?'

'Well I wan't going to hang around, was I. I just pissed off. Helped myself to a bit of redundancy money first, though.'

'Whaat!' says Ratface, 'Whaddaya mean? I mean how much did you take?'

'Ooh – not a lot. Not a lot considering all the work I've done for them. I knew the stingy bastards wouldn't give me nothing, I had to take it.'

'Eh! You can't go around nicking money! You'll have the police round here.'

'Phoo. They wouldn't call the police. They know I deserve it.'

'They'll never give you a reference now,' says Sue. 'How're you going to get another job without a reference?'

'How'm I going to get another job anyway? There aren't any, are there? What difference does it make?'

Ratface says: 'Don't worry about it. I'll put on a cup of tea. How about a joint to calm you down?'

'Yeah, ta. God, bloody Mr Bridges, you know what he said when he gave me the sack? "Blame it on the world recession." That's what they always say, isn't it?'

'The world recession! There's no world recession . . . Or if there is, 's only because of the arms race. Scrap the nuclear weapons programme and there'd be no more recession. It's simple, ridiculously simple, in fact. But meanwhile the politicians go on waffling and lying, they can't see that time's running out.'

'Thing that worries me is that they must be planning to use these bombs! I mean they go on about having a deterrent, but everyone knows they're no deterrent, I mean they didn't deter Argentina from attacking us did they? So they wouldn't deter a superpower . . .'

'Well at least you aren't paying for them any longer with your taxes,' says Ratface. 'That's why I'm proud to be on the dole. And that's another good thing about dope, eh Sue? At least you don't pay tax on it. I'm not giving any money to the Government, not so they can spend it on Cruise and Trident and all those other death-machines.' He lights up the joint.

'You reckon that justifies you smoking dope eh?' says Sue. 'Smoking dope's not going to help anyone. Not unless you believe in all that hippy "mind-expanding" crap, ha! Hmm, nothing's going to change for the better till women are in charge – stop men's fighting and stop men's aggression.'

'Hmm. Well, not all men are aggressive . . . Dope makes you non-aggressive!'

'Incapable . . .'

'And some women are very aggressive. Take Mrs Thatcher for instance . . . Phoo! You know I reckon the best thing that could happen would be for Mrs Thatcher to be given a joint of the old sinsemilla. Something to blow her out of her tree! Make her realise she's not Queen Boadicea and Winston Churchill rolled into one and stop playing macho politics, maybe she'd start doing something about the mess she's made . . .'

'Or make her resign, better still,' Dan suggests.

'Yeah, it might make her resign, mightn't it! I reckon dope's got all the answers.'

'I reckon you're cracked,' says Sue. 'Supposing – I mean, how'd you ever get this joint to Mrs Thatcher? Hahaha! Can you imagine? Post her a little number marked "Smoke Me" and hope for the best? You might as well send her a gun marked "Shoot Yourself" – get it over and done with.'

Dan laughs. 'You could get a whole stack of confiscated bushes from New Scotland Yard, make a bonfire in her back garden . . .'

'Make a bonfire in her bedroom, that's what I'd do.'

Ratface sighs again and starts playing with his bag of grass. He's trying to expel all the air from the bag, squeezing it with his fist, when suddenly there's a pop and a shower of grass lands on the table and in Sue's cup and all over the molten Ronald Reagan.

'Drugging Sue's tea now I see . . .'

'Oh fuckin' L, you're so clumsy . . . I don't know, all your big talk and you can't even get it together . . .'

Her voice trails off as Ratface scoops together as much of the grass as he can, and a bit of the ash, and a bit of the floor, and then attacks his packet of papers, pulling out more and more. 'Anyone want another smoke?' he asks when he's got about a dozen papers in front of him.

'God, what's it gonna be?' says Dan wide-eyed. 'You rolling us a chimney stack?'

'Well, *I* don't want another,' says Sue. 'I've got work to find, you know.'

But Ratface goes on rolling. 'I'm just doing a bit of stock-piling,' he explains. Within ten minutes he's rolled six bulging numbers, which he puts in the pocket of his donkey jacket. 'What are you doing today, Sue?'

'Oh, I've got some letters to write, I need to apply for a few jobs. . .'

'Dan?'

'Me? I'm feeling pretty wrecked actually. I might go and crash.'

Ratface shakes his head. 'Well *I* don't know. *I'm* not going to waste the day.' He stands up and looks out of the window. 'It's beautiful outside, I'm going out.' And he leaves the room.

Dan looks up when he hears the door shut. 'Eh? That was sudden . . . God, he must be crazy, it's fucking freezing out there.'

'Oh well, you know Ratface . . . changing the weather is nothing compared with changing the world.'

'Yeah, yeah.'

'I mean, he's got a box of matches, hasn't he. That's all you need when you're stoned out of your brain – a box of matches and a good imagination.'

# *Revelations*

Ratface is standing shivering at the bus-stop when he hears a familiar voice behind him. 'Well, hi, hello Ratty, how you doing!' He looks round and sees Harry grinning a toothless grin. Ratface grins back. 'Hi, hi! Fine, how are you?' They sway at each other for a few seconds. Harry's wearing a woollen hat pulled down over his ears, which frames his weatherbeaten face. His breath smells of alcohol.

'Where you going then, Ratty?'

'Just going home. I got chucked off the bus 'cos I didn't have enough money. I was trying to catch another, but . . .' He rubs his hands together. 'Looks like I'm out of luck.'

'Aye, they're hard to catch sometimes. Especially the single-deckers, you can't see 'em. Hey – d'you want to come back for a blow?'

'Yeah, never turn one down!'

'I've just been round to Martin's,' Harry explains. 'I just bought a record – the best record in the world! I tell you, it's a miracle, David Bowie's got nothing on this.'

'Yeah? Who's it by?'

'Oh, it's very valuable,' he says, producing a sleeveless 78 from his carrier-bag. 'This is worth lots of money, don't drop it,' and he promptly drops it into a puddle.

'Oh Harry, what are you doing? It's not going to be very valuable if you treat it like that!'

'Oh, I'll just give it a scrub when we get home, it'll be as good as new.'

Back at Harry's flat the door is wide open as usual. 'You

gotta meet Terry, you'll like Terry, he's a vegetable . . . vegarian, like you.' So Ratface is led into the far room, which is empty except for an armchair, a cheap music-centre, and a tall, skinny man who's sitting in the corner. The man stands up as they enter.

'Hey Terry, this is Ratty. Ratty, this is Terry.' Terry nods and stares. He looks like a sensitive sort of bloke, a bit nervous maybe, but his eyes look gentle and intelligent.

The door opens again and a girl of about 18 with bleached hair comes in. 'Hey Carol!' says Harry, 'I've gotta play this record. You'll love it, you'll not be able to believe it! Thirty years before reggy this is, probably Bob Marley listened to this, it's a collector's item.'

Carol takes the record and looks at it with contempt. 'Where d'you find this? In the skip?'

'Don't be crazy!' says Harry, snatching it back. 'Martin sold me this, it's a bargain, it's very valuable.'

'Don't be silly, you can't play that, it's a 78. We haven't got 78 on that stupid machine.'

'Well, I'll put it on 33 and 45, that must be about 78.' The needle skids across the record a few times before he manages to start it at the beginning.

'It's a bit slow isn't it?' says Carol.

'Well it lasts longer that way. You've got to imagine it faster – listen to that beat! Listen to that voice! It's like reggy isn't it, 30 years before reggy!'

Ratface tries to read the label as it spins round. 'James Foxton and the Amarillos – Blue Evening. Snappy, eh.'

'Sit down,' Harry tells him, indicating the chair. 'Don't worry, Carol won't sit there – says it's got bugs.'

Terry says: 'Tea?'

'Oh, yes please.' Ratface sits down and Terry leaves the room. Harry produces a lump of hash half the size of a Rubik's cube and skins up a joint.

As they puff away and listen to the record for the third time, Harry asks: 'So where'd you been today?'

'I went down to Piccadilly Circus.'

'Oh yes. To buy some drugs.'

'Er . . . No . . .'

'Oh what? To sell some drugs then.'

'Er – no.' How can be explain that he went there to try to give some stuff away, but couldn't find anyone to give it away to? After a long pause, he says: 'Er, d'you think . . . Have you ever thought . . . I don't know . . . That dope has powers, you know, to change your opinions, and alter your character, I mean in a positive way? Changing your attitudes and so on . . .'

'Oh yes. I'm all for that. I change *my* mind all the time, 'specially when I'm stoned.' Pause. 'But sometimes the whisky's like a vision too. That makes you appreciate good music, that does, the whisky.' The record grinds to a ponderous climax then stops. Harry decides to give the flip-side a spin, and at the same time turns up the volume. Carol gets up and leaves saying: 'You've been ripped off mate, why don't you admit it?' But Harry takes no notice, his eyes are shut and his whole body is moving in time with the music.

Ratface's mouth begins to feel dry, so rough and rasping that it hurts to swallow. But Terry's certainly taking his time.

Eventually the door opens again and Terry comes in with a tray which he puts down on the floor. 'Oh great, cuppa tea!' says Ratface, leaning forward. There are five cups on the tray but two of them are empty and the others are only half-full. He takes one of the fuller ones and has a sip. The tea is stone cold. God, has it been in the fridge or what? No wonder he's taken half an hour to make it. Harry doesn't even look at the tea. He gets up saying, 'I'm going to make a phone call' and leaves the room with Terry.

Ratface is quite relieved to be on his own, especially when the record comes to an end. His brain and ears relax, he's able to orientate himself and he decides he's not so stoned after all. Maybe he should have another smoke.

He's pondering the question when Terry comes back in, carrying a plate of mushy-looking brown beans. He sits down by the music-centre and starts picking at them tentatively.

'Harry says you're a vegetarian,' Ratface says. 'That looks nice.'

Terry doesn't say anything but holds the plate up to eye-level and stares at it. Ratface stares at it too, and wonders – Is he taking the piss? I mean, I know it doesn't actually look nice, it looks like a gooey mess. I just meant it looks *wholesome*. But Terry's face is too serious for him to be taking the piss. So is he offering me a bit? Should I take some? No, I can't snatch the plate from him and start munching away, that's not very good manners! Maybe he's inspecting the beans in the light, to see if any bugs are crawling on them; or maybe he's waiting for them to go cold, like the tea. Some vegetarians won't eat hot food. Terry's face doesn't give anything away.

Carol reappears smoking a cigarette. Noticing Ratty's puzzled expression, she explains: 'He's into yin and yang, you know – macrobiotics.'

Terry's face registers a little recognition and he produces a little booklet from his pocket. This time Ratface takes the offering. 'Oh yes,' he says, flicking through the pages. 'Yin and yang, I never quite understood that . . .' He finds a diagram. Pheasant and partridge and duck are very yang foods apparently; well, they're probably not very good for you. Beef and frog and asparagus are yin. Terry's eating his meal with obsessive care, picking at little bits, and then chewing every mouthful rigorously. 'What are those bits you're eating? Are those the yin parts?'

Terry looks up at him but goes on chewing.

'You know, I used to eat meat,' Ratface goes on, 'but one night I got really smashed and I was trying to cook some lamb chops. And I just started thinking, this is really repulsive, cooking the flesh of dead animals! Suddenly it all seemed really disgusting – you know, how would *I* like it if I ended up on somebody's plate! I couldn't eat meat after that . . . But it was being stoned, you know, it made me think completely differently. We've all been conditioned to eat animal flesh and well, for me, it was dope which made me overcome that conditioning.'

Terry looks up again, with a mystified expression on his face.

'Don't you agree? I think dope makes you forget all that negative conditioning, it helps you open your mind and work out things for yourself.' Terry stares hard at Ratface. 'No, don't you think? I mean – I was thinking earlier about what would happen if we gave Mrs Thatcher a joint. I think it'd be a revelation to her in some ways . . .'

Now Terry's brow is more furrowed than ever. Ratface is suddenly overcome with exasperation. Why won't he say anything? Am I just not explaining myself very well? 'All I mean is, what a difference it would be if everyone smoked, I reckon the world would be a much more relaxed place to live in.'

Terry's face lights up for a second, but then it goes blank again. He shakes his head and goes on picking at his food.

Ratface now feels completely confused. Am I so stoned that I don't realise how incoherent I'm being? It all seems pretty simple to me. In fact it *is* simple, put like that it's just naive, it's all total drivel. He's beginning to feel depressed; if someone like Terry doesn't think it's worth speaking to him, how's he ever going to get through to the general public?

The silence is broken by Terry mumbling something in a high-pitched voice.

'Sorry, I didn't catch that,' Ratty says; but Terry just looks confused again. What's the matter? Is he foreign or deaf or something maybe? Terry puts aside his plate and leaves the room. Ratface wonders whether to ask Carol 'What's up with him?' but she'd probably turn round and say: 'What's up with *you*, more like, you doped out old hippy. It's you who's been spouting rubbish all evening!' So he says nothing.

When Terry returns he's carrying a plateful of brown doughy-looking lumps. Some macrobiotic dessert perhaps? But no, when he's shown the lumps he realises they're bits of modelling clay. He picks up one of them and begins to knead it. 'Yeah, great. What're you going to make with this?'

'Sssh!' whispers Carol. 'That's the finished product! Those are his sculptures!'

'Oh shit!' He quickly puts down the lump he's been kneading. 'I've just ruined one of them.' He tries to put it back into shape, wondering: What the hell are they sculptures of? Dog shit? 'Er – they're very interesting. Very unusual.'

Terry gives another little squeaky speech and resumes his painstaking meal.

'He does a lot of sculpting, he writes poetry too,' says Carol. 'He sees flying saucers and stuff.'

'Oh what, you've seen flying saucers?'

Terry nods and smiles for the first time. 'Nnnnnnnn.'

'You know, I've never seen any myself. But I'm not saying they don't exist. Have you seen flying saucers here, in London?'

He nods again and makes an expressive flourish with his arms.

'Everywhere huh?' Terry starts staring at all the corners of the room in turn. Yeah. I see. Acid, eh. It's a shame when someone reckons he's found reality in a piece of blotting paper. An even greater shame when you open some doors and find that some others have slammed behind you for ever. Ratface doesn't know what more to say. He squirms in his seat and wonders whether he should leave.

Now the door flies open again. 'WHA-A-AT happened to my record then? Who took off my record? I want a blow, who'll give me a blow?!' Harry's carrying a can of beer, and there's another bulging in his pocket. 'Now where's my record . . .'

Carol leaps up and pushes him to the ground. 'No, no, not that bloody record! I couldn't stand it!'

But Harry manages to get up and put the record on. 'It's great, isn't it?' he says to Ratface as he swigs his beer. 'Here, why don't you roll up a number.'

Ratface obliges although he doesn't really feel in a party mood. The joint makes him feel even more like a wet teabag. Sue's words come back to him: she was so cross with him earlier, saying such nasty things, about how lazy he was and then 'I'd rather live with a bunch of speedfreaks than a burnt-out old hippy like you,' that's what she said wasn't it? And him only 24 and hardly burnt out and hardly a hippy either, although his hair *is* getting a bit long and he likes Neil Young and old Jefferson Airplane records. But a mindless old hippy, no no no! He does have principles, after all! He doesn't smoke dope to "escape from reality" or to keep him in a permanently lazy hazy state – but he does enjoy it, and he doesn't see why the police and the judges should forbid him to do what he enjoys. He resents this very much, first thing in the morning and last thing at night. Every time he lights a joint, and especially when he's sharing one, he feels he's carrying on his quiet crusade against authority.

But at the moment he feels lost. Terry's staring into space; Carol's reading an old scrap of newspaper and looking fed up. He tries chatting to Harry but can't get much response. Suddenly it occurs to him: Harry's obviously tripping too! And then a second later – I must be tripping as well! There must've been something in the dope or in the tea! His brain does a triple somersault and lands upside-down. Carol puts on a Roxy Music record, so loud that it pounds in his ears and sounds truly demonic. Oh *why* did I go to Piccadilly Circus today, smoking in front of all those policemen, am I going crazy? And words spoken earlier in the day come back to him as grotesque parodies, the quintessence of idiocy.

At last he turns to Harry and says: 'I feel really out of it, you know.'

'Oh, have another smoke if you want,' Harry replies. He's swigging from the second can now and at the same time using it as an ashtray.

'Oh no, no, I tell you, I'm really smashed.' He gets up slowly, unsure of whether he can still stand. 'Well, bye then.' He's not even confident enough to say the ritual 'Drop by whenever you want'. He feels totally drained.

'Bye then.'

Outside, the roads are almost empty. A strong, dry wind is

blowing as he heads back towards the flat. All the way home he keeps his eyes fixed to the ground, not daring to look up for fear of what he might see in the night sky. Oh God, oh God, not while my brain is stewed – don't let me see any flying saucers tonight!

# *Thursday*

## *The end of the line*

Spring is definitely here at last. The sun is shining, the passers-by are talking to each other rather than to themselves, and the musty cideros are sitting on the steps of the Job Centre.

Sue's heart sinks in anticipation as she goes inside. She goes through this ritual three times a week, sometimes more, and yet this morning she received a letter telling her that her dole was about to be cut off and that she must find a job. That easy, eh? 'Find a job.' She feels like going up to one of the desks and giving an earful to the smug little man behind it. You cretin, do you think I haven't tried to find work? Do you think now I can just snap my fingers and get a job? I'm not the only one, you know – don't you read the papers? Go on, then, find me a job, if you think it's so easy! It'd be a waste of time though, she knows what the answer would be – 'Go and join the queue at Door 8 if you have any queries.'

She starts at the Temporary and Part-Time section. Only one vacancy today – 'Part-timer wanted by travel centre. Must be fluent in Swahili.' She moves on to 'Drivers' – 'Chauffeur wanted for elderly couple. Must have own Rolls.' It's always the bloody same, isn't it. She looks around her and wonders: How come everyone else can keep their cool in here? How come everyone's always so quiet and miserable? How come no one ever wants to kick up a fuss? They're all bruised and beaten, I suppose, on their best behaviour trying to impress the staff. As if the staff give a shit about any of them. There's no help ever, no advice or encouragement; just 'All the jobs we have are on display' and 'Sorry, that one's already been filled.'

A scrawny old man, with strings of snot hanging from his nose, is looking at the catering jobs. That poor old sod'll never find a job in a kitchen, not if he can't keep his own nose clean. He's muttering and pulling faces as he staggers along. Probably even Camden Council, the Equal Opportunity Employers, don't make provisions for people like that. God, how can people believe in souls and an afterlife, aren't there enough wretched miserable people around already without consigning everyone to eternal life? That poor devil . . . I mustn't sneer at him, I'll be like that myself one day – yeah, and I'll probably still be here, living out my last days in this ratshit hole. I mean, that's what the Government keeps on telling us, that most school-leavers today will never have a job. So that either means we'll all be on the dole until we retire, or they've got other plans for us. Probably they've got other plans for us. They'll never miss us anyway – the girl with the mohican and the bloke with the tea-towel draped around his shoulders and the frumpy woman with the moustache – they won't be using any of us in their plans to build a Master Race.

Now, let's see if there're any new office jobs . . . Filing clerk, that'd be a doss, but – 'Must have three years' experience.' Don't know why, for fuck's sake. I know my alphabet, I can pull out a drawer without setting your teeth on edge, I even know how to move a full filing cabinet (you take out the drawers first). I could bluff my way through maybe, but these bastards here know I've had no office experience apart from signing on once a month.

'Girl Friday wanted. Exempted vacancy. Must be adaptable and have a sense of humour' – i.e. mustn't complain about sexual harrassment. No, I'm not going to fuel the ego of some ageing executive. Ugh! I'd rather sell my body on the streets, at least then I'd be my own boss. And what about this. 'Vivacious receptionist wanted.' They obviously want a dolly-bird too, whoever heard of a man being described as vivacious?

The telephone starts ringing. None of the lazy sods behind the desks look like they're going to answer it, either.

The restaurant jobs are just as bad. 'Waitress wanted, Female/male.' I'm not going to fall for that one, they'd probably make me wear a slit skirt and fishnet tights. 'Exclusive businessmen's club requires attractive barstaff.' Sorry, I don't have an O-level in attractiveness, at school they didn't tell me how much it was going to matter.

A tall, gaunt man walks by, and Sue thinks: For sure he's a rapist. He has the eyes of a rapist. Now, it's easy to see why *he* wouldn't be any good as a receptionist . . . He'd be in too much competition with the boss! She moves along, out of his view.

From where she's standing now she can see that there's no one at the desk on which the telephone is ringing. Still, what's everyone else doing? Is the entire staff equipped with ear-plugs or are they all filling in their football pools coupons? If they're so busy here, as they always say, why don't they just employ more people? Burr-burr! Burr-burr! Christ, and they call *us* lazy! Anyone could do this job!

Sue glowers at the man sitting nearest the phone – no wonder he's not moving, he's so fat he must need a pulley to lift him from his seat. Sue becomes incensed by his blotchy face and sullen features . . . He's just staring at a piece of paper! Suddenly her temper bursts. She strides across the room to the telephone, picks up the receiver and says: 'Hello? Misery Centre. Can I help you?'

She's all set to take down a message when the receiver is whipped from her grasp and she flinches, expecting a clout across the head. But the man who grabbed it simply gives her an exasperated look before assuming his oiliest voice to say down the receiver: 'Hello? Job Centre. I'm very sorry about that, we're having a bit of trouble with some of the youngsters . . .'

Sue raises her hands in frustrated rage, does a half-turn and notices that a middle-aged woman behind another desk is staring at her, horrorstruck. She rushes over to her and says: 'What's the matter? No one else wanted to answer it.'

The woman continues to gape in silence, so she goes on: 'I

was just trying to get a bit of work experience, if you like. I thought it might be my big break! I thought someone might discover me and give me a job.'

'Don't be insolent,' the woman retorts in a prim, plummy voice. 'I've never seen such a display in my entire life. What an outburst!'

Never seen such a display? Well, I can do much better than that . . . But her anger subsides for a moment, and she picks up what the clerk is saying over the telephone: 'Yes, yes . . . I know . . . Diabolical . . . Luckily most of the people who come here are surprisingly well-behaved, but of course we also get the rabble, the delinquents . . .'

Unemployable, completely unemployable.

Sue's temper rises again – what does he mean anyway, *surprisingly* well-behaved? What does he expect the unemployed to be like, a bunch of savages? I could show him what a savage behaves like! She feels like spitting in his face . . . But why live up to his expectations?

She looks again at 'Thunderstruck, Surrey' and tries to assume a tone of pride and disgust. 'I only came looking for work. I was using a bit of initiative, that's all.'

'No wonder you can't find a job,' she replies. 'You have no self-discipline.'

Well, that's plainly absurd. Sue feels she's exercising the self-discipline of a saint, considering the circumstances. What more can you say to these stupid people? She turns and marches off. She's feeling two feet taller than everyone around her, although she doesn't dare look at anyone for fear of discovering that she's really two foot shorter. Her heart's beating fast as she steps out onto the street. Thank God for some sunlight! Thank God for some air and some noise! It's just a shame that I'll have to walk twice as far to look for jobs in future – I'll not be coming here again!

Dan's parking his bike when she gets back to the flat. 'Hi, where've you been?' she calls out to him.

'Jesus Christ, don't ask me. I've been down the dole office.'

'What? Yeah? That's where I just been myself – well, the Job Centre. Oh, you've been registering unemployed, of course. What happened?'

'Bloody disaster, wasn't it. Bloody joke. They told me to fill in some forms and then they gave me a number and they just kept me waiting. For hours and hours and hours. I was down there for more than three hours, d'you realise? I worked out that if they carried on at the rate they were going, they wouldn't see me until two o'clock tomorrow afternoon. In the end I just couldn't stand it any longer, I got up and left. I was so angry.' Sue opens the front door of the flat. 'D'you think that was silly of me?'

'No, I know how you feel. But that's their *game*, isn't it. That's exactly what they *want* people to do – get so demoralised that they don't bother claiming their rights! But you've got to fight against it, it's your duty. It's your duty to register . . . to get all you can.'

'Yeah, yeah, I suppose . . . Maybe.'

'No, go on. Go back now. You can't let 'em beat you like this.'

'Oh what? Now?'

'Yeah! Yeah! Go on. And you mustn't play their game this time. You mustn't lose your temper.'

What else can you do?

# *Outlooks*

Ratface is hanging up some net curtains in the kitchen and listening to a current-affairs programme on the radio. A male politician has spent the last three minutes evading a question on the economy. 'I think it should be palpably obvious to everyone who has unrestricted access to the genuine facts . . . I think this is not the real question we should be examining at the moment . . . I think . . .' I think I think I don't think. Holy shit this is mind-numbing – my brain's going to seize up and die if I have to listen to much more of this. Let's have some pop music instead.

He's retuning the radio when there's a knock at the front door. He turns down the volume and strains his ears – it's not the police, is it? He hears Sue open the door and say, 'Ah hello Mrs Watkins, John's in the kitchen.' Then Sue's bedroom door slams shut again.

He quickly puts the curtains on a chair and brushes the hair away from his eyes. 'Mum,' he says as she comes in, 'you didn't say you were coming round.'

'I just dropped by. I was passing, and I thought I'd drop off some letters which arrived for you at Glebe Road . . . nothing very important, I don't think.'

She hands her son half-a-dozen letters and a couple of large brown envelopes. He flicks through but doesn't open any of them.

'Yes, thanks a lot. Doesn't look like there's anything very exciting, but thanks anyway.' Now he's stuck for anything more to say. His mother is standing in silence too, so he says:

'Are you in a rush to get somewhere? Would you like a cup of tea?'

'Oh yes please.' She puts down her bag and sits down. Ratface washes up some cups, and dries them, and rinses out the teapot, all especially carefully because he wants his mum to see how domesticated he's become, and because the longer he's at the sink the longer he's got to think of something to say.

'Still no sign of a job yet?' Mrs Watkins asks when he eventually sits down.

He sighs. 'Honestly there's nothing around. I keep my eyes open but you know, it's really discouraging. Remember there's four million other people looking for work too . . .'

'*Three* million, in fact. And that's an inflated figure. *Three* million people, *pretending* to look for work. I should've thought that for an intelligent boy like you . . . If only you'd cut your hair and try to look a bit respectable.'

'Look it's not a question of that! How can anyone tell what length my hair is when I speak on the phone? You can't even get an interview these days, it's impossible.'

'Perhaps you're too fussy. I'm sure if you didn't mind what you were doing and what you were paid, you could find a job . . .'

'Look, there really isn't anything!' Ratface raises his voice in frustration. 'It's not a question of *me* being fussy, it's the employers who're being fussy! You should go down to the Job Centre and see for yourself . . . And you know, people are being made redundant every day, Dan lost his job just yesterday.'

'Well that's hardly surprising with the way he dresses, in that old motorbike jacket all the time.'

'Look, it's not *like* that – there *is* no bloody work!'

He doesn't often swear in front of his mother, but this time he feels he's got a point and he wants to ram it home. Mrs Watkins promptly shuts up.

At last she says: 'Still, I'm sure there are jobs around if you really looked, made an effort to make yourself look presentable.'

Ratface doesn't know how he can make his point any clearer. He'd definitely never say 'fucking' to his mother, although he did let it slip out once in the middle of a blazing row many years ago when she caught him smoking cigarettes. He'd like her to think he's too mature to say such a thing now . . . that life on the dole has turned him into a sober, responsible citizen.

He says: 'Anyway, how'm I meant to look presentable on twenty quid a week? How can I buy clothes on that?'

'Now that's a very weak excuse. You don't need expensive clothes to look smart. You've got some perfectly good clothes at Glebe Road, I keep on telling you.'

Ratface pours out the tea which has been brewing. What clothes at Glebe Road? He tries to remember what his pitiful wardrobe contains – a few nylon shirts with outsize collars, a kipper tie, a dark polyester suit which is so threadbare that it shines all over like grey lamé. 'Oh mum, that stuff looks *so* scruffy.'

'Not half as scruffy as what you've got on,' she snaps back. Ratface falls silent now, and Mrs Watkins starts inspecting her surroundings. 'So how do you keep yourself busy these days?' she asks.

'Well, there's always lots to be done . . . washing, cooking . . .' Perfecting the art of making tea. 'Shopping . . .' He always seems to be going up to the shops for matches or skins or chocolate. 'I'm not a layabout, I'm always doing stuff around the house.'

His eyes fall involuntarily on the net curtains which are draped over the chair.

'What are you doing with those?' his mother enquires.

'Mm, I was just about to put them up.'

'Put them up! I thought you must be taking them down. Whoever heard of lace curtains in the kitchen!' Ratface sighs as she goes on, 'Have you been putting them up in the other rooms, in your bedroom too I suppose?'

'Yes, I found them in the cupboard, I thought we might as well use them.'

'It's all part of the vanity of youth, of course. The young are so vain they imagine that people are always looking at them. Why do you think everyone's so interested in you?'

'No, I don't think everyone's so interested . . .'

'Lace curtains are so . . . genteel,' she pronounces, and Ratface thinks: Who's talking about *lace* anyway, you've got to be rich to be able to afford lace curtains.

Mrs Watkins hasn't touched her tea at all yet, but now that it's almost cold she drains it in three or four gulps.

'Well, I mustn't invade your privacy any longer,' she says pointedly. Ratface stares back at her as she stands up. 'I do wish you'd go to the hairdressers. Make yourself a bit more employable. An intelligent lad like you, shouldn't be sitting around doing nothing.'

'I don't do nothing . . .' Hang on, that's not grammatical is it? It should be I don't do anything, no hang on . . . 'I do try.'

'Well it's nice to catch a glimpse. Drop by if you can. And don't give up hope of finding a job, will you?'

She turns to go and Ratface follows her down the passage saying: 'Yes, nice to see you, thanks for the letters, are you alright, well bye-bye then.'

Sue emerges from her bedroom as he's walking back to the kitchen. 'Oops, sounded like a bit of grilling there,' she says.

'Yeah, and you weren't much help were you? I wanted you to come and back me up, tell her how impossible it is to find a job.'

'Why would she believe me if she doesn't believe you?'

'Well, because you dress smartly, because you've got short hair, because you're a girl, because you go down to the Job Centre every other day.'

'I was going to come and rescue you but I wasn't expecting her to leave so soon. I was reading something in *Around Town* . . . Look, You and Your Bright Ideas! are playing at the Underground tonight, I bet we could blag our way in.'

'You and Your Bright Ideas!? I've never seen them. I heard that single they gave you.'

' "Pinstriped"? Yeah, they're better live. Last time I saw

them was at the Blue Anchor, they really ripped the place apart.'

'Think I'd like them? Oh well, if you think we could get in for free . . . Could give it a go . . .' He stares blankly at the table, then notices his pile of letters and begins tearing them open. His eagerness quickly changes to disappointment. 'Great, gardening catalogue . . . What's this, Congratulations you have won a prize? Shit, it's just a lucky number for a draw. Where do all these mail-order people get my name from, I'd like to know?' He looks out of the window to make sure his mother is out of sight, then picks up his net curtains.

'Ha! Your mum didn't go for them much, did she.'

'No, did you hear that? What a fuss, eh . . . That was a bit close to the bone too, I thought – "No one's at all interested in you", that's a nice thing to be told by your own mother! Oh shit . . . Now she's going to tell all her friends how fraightfully genteel John has become, mmm, how "insufferably bourgeois"!'

'Well, she did say you should become respectable. I'd've thought lace curtains was the height of respectability.'

'Well you'd've thought so . . .'

'So why *are* you putting those things up?'

'Why? Why d'you think? So that people can't see the crop of course! I don't want passers-by to see that we're growing a dangerous crop of illegal plants!'

'Oh, I'd forgotten about the crop . . . I suppose it's planting time again, isn't it.'

'The seeds have just started sprouting, I gotta show you. Hang on.' He trots off to his bedroom and returns with a tobacco tin which he's lined with cotton-wool. 'Here they are, the little treasures! See their pretty little faces! Remarkable I think . . . Humph, and my mum saying "No one's interested in what you do". The police would be pretty interested, wouldn't they? I'm just taking some sensible precautions.'

'I bet your mum would be proud to know what a sensible young man you've become.'

'In my old age.' He tucks up the seeds again in the cotton-wool bed, then tackles the net curtains for the third time. This time he succeeds in getting them up.

'Bang goes my television screen,' is Sue's comment. 'Now I can't look out on the street.'

'You can draw them for the moment if you want.'

'What, and look like some nosey old bag or a peeping tom?'

Sue sighs, tries to look out of the window but just gets an eyeful of netting. 'God – talk about paranoid.'

'You complain now, but I bet you'll be smoking the crop with us when it comes up.'

'That's the least I deserve after all this trouble.'

'Well, I guess if we're going out this evening I'd better start getting ready.' He produces his stash and his skins and starts rolling up another batch of joints. Sometimes he feels like a worker on a factory production-line; joint-rolling can be a repetitive and time-consuming business. 'And after this I've got to do my washing. And I've got to go to the Post Office. And I promised I'd call round on Nick. I don't know, there's so much to do . . . I don't know where some people find the time.'

# *On the mend*

There's a dilemma here. Should you thrash the hell out of your bike when it's new, or should you treat it gently and prepare it for a long and happy old age? In a violent world, in which the future is uncertain, it could be argued that you should enjoy it while you've got it. But economy and good sense tells Dan to treat his bike as if he expects it to last for years.

Dan treated his last machine with the utmost care and respect. He used to clean it regularly, feed it with the right fuel and maintain it throughout. In the winter he even covered it with a blanket at night to protect it from the cold and ice. He always made sure that it was in perfect condition, and refused to hurl it about like Rick and Jerry did with their bikes. They thought he was strange, but he used to tell himself – 'My bike will still be going at 50, 60, 70 thousand miles when theirs are rotting on the scrapheap.'

Then one day he went downstairs and found that his gleaming machine had been transformed into a charred mess, a sad skeleton standing in two pools of molten rubber. He was totally heartbroken and didn't get over the loss for weeks. It was insured, luckily; but he couldn't persuade the insurance company that it was a beautifully cared-for machine with new tyres and a perfect engine with years of life in it. So he got £200, the same as if he'd completely neglected it all its life, done nothing but batter and abuse it.

Soon afterwards he found work at Prewitt's Booking Agency in the West End, and was able to buy a new 175 cc trail bike. He intended to look after it; but he found that his job took up all his time, and it was quite impossible to do much more than fill it with petrol and tighten the chain occasionally. Six mornings a week he'd have to ride into town like a maniac so as not to be late, and in the evening he'd be too knackered to do anything except ride home again like a maniac and slump down at the kitchen table. Someone could've cut his brake cables or loosened all the bolts on his front wheel, and he'd never have known until it was too late. Sometimes it occurred to him that he might be deliberately tempting providence, that he was in fact trying to kill himself to be free from the tedium of his job; but in the end all it boiled down to was that he had no time or energy. And so he realised it was true: that work can seriously damage your health.

But now he's suddenly got lots of time on his hands. Time to make a new resolution. Time to look after himself and his bike – his poor, neglected little bike. Never again, he promises, will he be so careless.

He finishes tightening the drive-chain. There, my baby, that'll feel better. And then there's the spark-plugs to check . . . and the tyres . . . and the brakes . . . and the timing . . . and the whole thing needs a good polish. He won't be able to do it all today, because it'll be getting dark soon; but he must change the engine oil tonight. Before the whole bloody thing seizes up.

He finds an empty paint tin and drains the old oil into it. Fine, the tin's just big enough. But now – what's he to do with it? It's illegal to pour it into the sewers, and the lid won't fit because it's all encrusted with paint. He'll have to take it down to the garage and let them dispose of it, they're sure to have facilities for this sort of thing. So he packs up his tools and sets off on foot, holding the tin carefully so that he doesn't spill any of it, and looking round a few times (as if he's still on the bike) afraid that a passing jogger might career into him and send the whole lot flying.

It's pleasant to be able to take a leisurely stroll anyway. Not to be in a rush to get somewhere. What was it Rat was talking about yesterday – about 'The Fifth Freedom', the Freedom of

Time. Walking's good for the body . . . it's good for the brain, too. Though I wish I could get that bloody Bananarama song out of my head.

When he reaches the garage at last the attendant looks at him with wide-eyed surprise.

'I'd like to get rid of this,' Dan says. 'Have you got anywhere I can pour it away?'

'Oh no,' he replies. 'That wouldn't do at all, if everyone just came and dumped their oil with us.'

'But what am I meant to do with it then?'

'Do what you like. That's your own business.'

So with a surge of frustration Dan walks away again. What am I meant to do with the bloody stuff then? I can do what I like with it can I? Oh well, in that case . . . And he empties the whole lot into the gutter and watches the thick black slime trickle down the road. Silly me, why didn't I think of that in the first place? Oh well, I'll know next time.

When he turns around to go home he's horrified to see a young besuited man running towards him and waving. He blushes guiltily, and is even more taken aback when the man grins and says, 'Daniel old mate! Fancy seeing you here! What're you up to these days?'

'Bloody hell! Peter! God you've changed. God you gave me a fright. What are you doing here?'

'I was filling up my car.' He points to a little red hatchback on the forecourt. 'I thought it was you.' He holds out his hand.

Dan puts the paint tin on the ground, wipes his hand on his jeans and then shakes Peter's hand awkwardly. Peter has a strong, confident grip. He's become a handsome bastard, too. Dan suddenly feels scruffy and inferior.

'I'm sure you've got lots to tell me,' Peter goes on. 'It's been ages, hasn't it. Look, we must get together some time.'

'Yeah, yeah.'

'How about tomorrow? We should meet for a drink. What about the Old Lion in Blackmore Street, d'you know it? They serve Bishops.'

'Blackmore Street? I'll find it.'

'Splendid, splendid. Eight o'clock alright for you? Excellent. Well I must say, this is a nice surprise, isn't it? But I must rush now, I have a dinner party this evening and I have to get ready. See you tomorrow then.' And he scurries back to his car.

Thank you, thinks Dan, I don't need a lift; I'd hate to dirty your nice clean seats. He picks up the paint tin and heads back home.

# *Keeping the peace*

The doorman shakes his head and holds up a crumpled scrap of paper. 'Well, you're not on the guest list. Friends of the band, you reckon? Who d'you know exactly?'

Sue says: 'Linda's an old friend, she always gets me in for free.'

'Who's Linda?'

'She's lead singer with You and Your Bright Ideas!'

The doorman pushes the swing-door behind him and bellows above the din – 'Hey, Rog! Come here!' Rog appears in a Muscle tee-shirt. 'Hey Rog. What's the bird called in You and Your Bright Ideas!?'

'Uh, search me . . . Pauline wasn't it?'

'Linda, Linda,' Sue prompts, but Rog looks blank.

Now Ratface steps forward. 'You've got to let us in,' he says. 'We've got some essential supplies for the band.' He digs into his jacket pocket and flashes a couple of slightly bent joints, half-concealed in the palm of his hand.

Rog nods. 'What about essential supplies for the security staff? I hope you remembered them too.'

Ratface dutifully produces another couple of joints and gives them to the doorman, who puts them in his cashbox and says 'Next!' although there's no one else in the queue.

The support band is tuning up between numbers as Sue and Ratface file in. About 20 people are watching the stage, more are standing at the bar. Ratface looks at the band, and is pleased to see that no ears are visible onstage. He grew up at a time when a rock star's ears were seen as seldom as his granny, and he's not in favour of today's fashion of elevating every sundry gormless wimp to star status. A rock star should look like a rock star, he thinks, not a bloody chemistry student.

'What are this lot called?' he says, as the bass and drums start pounding away at a promising prelude to destruction.

'Dunno, they're crap. I'm gonna see if Linda's arrived yet, wanna come?'

'No thanks, I think I'll watch this lot.' He has to shout to make himself heard as a wailing guitar breaks in. 'Here, you'd better take these joints. I've still got a bunch more.'

Thunder down the road
Don't worry 'bout the load
Burn along the track
The devil's on my back.

Sue gives him a disparaging look, takes the joints and then picks her way through the crowd to the changing-room. 'Friend of Linda's' she tells the man in a dark suit by the door. He waves his thumb to indicate that she can go in.

She opens the door tentatively and Bruce, the vulturine drummer, says: 'God, here's a groupie.'

'No room,' says another male voice from behind the door. But Linda springs up and kisses Sue on the cheek and says: 'Sue, great to see you, you should've told us and we'd've put you on the guest list.'

'Don't worry, got in for free anyway.'

'Oi, it's bastards like you who make sure we never get any money for these gigs. Did anyone pay to get in tonight?' Seymour is adjusting his guitar-strap. 'I feel like playing it low and mean tonight,' he says, swigging from his can of beer.

'Don't worry about him,' Linda says. 'Sit down won't you.' She has a motherly, efficient manner; she's over 40 and doesn't look a day younger. 'It's a bit of a squeeze, isn't it? Hey Bruce, you sure this is the dressing-room, not the broom cupboard?'

'Course I am, there's no broom in this dump! Think this

might be the toilet though, I've been watching out for people coming in for a slash against the wall . . .'

'There's obviously a tradition,' says Sue with a sniff. She begins to examine the graffiti on the wall in front of her, but it's a bit disappointing. "Merry." "Smurf." "Which ones the ref." "Speak and spit will play the Rainbow".'

'Have you met our new bassist?' Linda says. 'Sue, this is Tracie . . . Sue.'

They exchange hi's and Sue thinks Tracie's attractive, isn't she – huge eyes and thick black hair piled back in a shock. 'When did you join the band?'

'Oh, about two months ago, but I've been playing bass for longer. Before this I was in a band called the Resisters, 'dyou hear of 'em?' But Sue shakes her head and Tracie does too. 'Only played about two gigs . . .'

'Mind you, it's not hard to see why,' Linda breaks in, 'we've never had so much trouble at our gigs since she joined the band.'

'How d'you mean?'

Tracie tuts and casts her eyes upwards, so Linda explains – 'You know, just all these creepy blokes shouting things, you know, offensive things, directed at Tracie. Drunks rushing onto the stage and trying to touch her or kiss her.'

'That creep with the Union Jack on his head, he did kiss me! Disgusting. If I hadn't been playing a song at the time I'd have had my fingers round his bloody neck.'

'It's funny, isn't it, it's warped . . . After all the Rock Against Sexism gigs we've done and we still get these stupid yahoos coming along.'

'Maybe it's the support bands you pick,' Sue suggests, as another tortuous guitar-break wails through the walls.

'Don't blame us,' says Bruce, 'blame the manager, he's standing outside if you want him. Making sure we don't escape.'

'I thought punk was meant to change all this,' says Linda. 'Know what I mean? Put an end to all these axe-heroics, all this macho rock posing . . . Oi, Tracie . . . What about that gig you were at in St Albans, when that bloke came up to you . . .'

'Ugh, at the Green Man! That was a few years ago, mind. I was just standing watching this punk band, 'dyou ever hear of the Backstabbers?'

'Mm, no . . .'

'Well anyway, I was just standing watching this band, minding my own business, and this greasy bloke comes up to me and says "Do you?" I didn't know what he meant, "Do you have a light?" or something maybe. Well I didn't know. And he leered at me and said "Do you?" again, and then he started feeling me, ugh! Touching me! I was so embarrassed I just left. Course I was a lot younger then – now I'd have bloody clobbered him! Ripped his knackers off.'

'So what did he mean?' Sue asks. 'Do you?'

'Well, I found out a bit later. Apparently one of the gutter papers had just done this story on punk rock, saying that if you went up to a "punkette" at a gig, and said "Do you?", she'd just say, "Okay", and take you into the Ladies and suck you off.'

'Ooh, gross!'

'Makes you sick, dunnit! Bloody gutter press, bloody male fantasies. And now when I'm onstage it's almost as bad. The boys in the audience all think I'm available or something, just because all male rock stars are only after one thing, they think I must be desperate too. So insulting . . .'

'A lot more people are interested in the band since Tracie joined,' says Linda. '*The Sun* rang up last week, wanted to do a picture of her – topless.'

'I just yelled PISS OFF at them down the phone. That's so degrading.'

'The paper that supports our boys – the paper that humiliates my sisters, more like. You know, one of the reasons I formed this band, one of the reasons I felt strongly about fronting it, is that when women reach my age, you know, they're ignored. Forgotten. This society only wants glamorous young women, they don't want to look at you when you're beyond a certain age. So I formed this band thinking – Well, they're going to have to look at me! So what happens? Three years of nil exposure and then we get a dolly-bird on bass and suddenly everyone wants to know us . . . Sorry dear,' she says, patting Tracie on the knee, 'I don't mean to be rude.'

'You getting a lot of interviews then?'

'Well, there was some bloke from a Dutch fanzine the other week,' says Bruce, who's trying to juggle with his drumsticks.

'Tell the truth I don't really care about interviews,' Linda says. 'The music press is really stupid. I mean, we did this interview for *Music Mirror* a while back – did you see it? Christ, when I saw it I wanted to go out and burn every single copy. It made us out to be a bunch of staring halfwits. See, we'd been giving all this political rap, talking about sexism and nuclear weapons and the Tories and so on. Unfortunately the interviewer decided to leave out the political content completely. So the article was just full of all the dullest details possible – "Bruce taps his fingers and yawns. Linda says oh dear look at the time. Seymour picks his nose and has a swig of beer".'

Seymour looks up suspiciously when he hears his name. 'What was that? I heard that.'

'Just telling Sue here how you'll be the next to go.'

'What. Oh, thanks. Actually I've been wondering how to break it to you that I decided to quit. I'm making a bid for stardom on my own.'

This puts an end to the conversation for a while. Sue's wondering whether she should leave them in peace, but doesn't much fancy witnessing the dying throes of the support band.

Linda bends forward and hunts around in the bag at her feet. 'I've got something for you. It's our first release with the new line-up, it should be in the shops around now. Here, it's yours, we've got stacks of them.'

Seymour butts in, 'Hey, we can't afford to give them away.' But Linda says, 'Sssh. I'll pay for it then. Go on, Sue.'

She takes the single. On the front there's a picture of a mud-caked World War One soldier: 'Non-Essential Personnel b/w Pinstriped Dub Mix.'

'Look at the words,' Linda urges, so she turns it over and reads – 'All tracks written and published by You and Your Bright Ideas! Copyright.'

When times are tough for the ruling classes
They sit around on their fat arses
Discussing how to quell the masses.

(Hmm, is that 'asses' or 'marses', I wonder?)

And in the end they all decide
To take the people for a ride
And tell us God is on our side.
They wave their flags and tell a story
About the power and the glory
They say you must die to be free
And send them off across the sea
To kill each other in the mud
And vanish in a sea of blood.

Outside, the music reaches a thrashing crescendo and then dies suddenly. There are a few claps, a couple of cheers.

I hope they've got their own dressing-room, thinks Sue, otherwise I'm off. She carries on reading –

When times are sticky for our leaders
Beware of all the crap they'll feed us
They'll tell us how oppression freed us.

'How does the tune go?'

'It's quite catchy, in fact. There's a good bass-line; well, you'll hear it. But I don't like to drown out the words, I think they're very important.'

'That's why she's printed them on the sleeve,' says Bruce. 'Personally I think she should've printed the drum solo on the sleeve.'

'Hey Seymour, if you're going out, get us another can of beer! I'm not even drunk yet.'

'We'll be going on in 20 minutes,' says Linda. 'Give the crew time to set up the stage. Build up a bit of atmosphere.' There's another awkward silence.

'Shouldn't I leave you to get ready?' Sue asks Linda. 'Don't you have to gargle or something?'

'Not tonight, I left my razor-blades at home.'

'Oh, hold on, I've got something else you can gargle on.' Now it's her turn to fumble around. She produces Ratty's spliffs and says: 'D'you want to light up these?'

'Well, seeing as there's no one from the music press here. . .' Linda smiles, lights up one of the joints, and gives Tracie the other.

'Bloody music press,' says Bruce, stretching out his hand in anticipation. 'See you with a Rizla packet and they'll call you an ageing hippy.'

'Mind you, there's enough of *them* in the audience tonight – ageing hippies I mean,' Seymour has just returned from the bar and is passing round more cans. 'Wrought Iron has brought them out of the woodwork.'

'Wrought Iron, is that what they're called?!' Linda throws back her head and laughs.

'Fuckin' L,' says Tracie, 'Ageing hippies in the audience, what're we going to do, Lin? Maybe we should change our name for the night, become You and Your Leaden Ideas! Know what I mean?'

Ratface brushes the hair away from his eyes. Wrought Iron? Mmm. Silly name. Not such bad songs though, at least they've got a bit of guts unlike most of the drivel on the radio these days. They must've been good, he hasn't even had a smoke yet! Now, though, he feels the urge so he takes out his supply of numbers and studies them. 'Three big ones, two little ones . . . No point keeping them all to myself.' He lights up the big ones, keeps one for himself, and passes the others off into the throng. Three clouds of sweet-smelling smoke waft into the air.

Ratface is enjoying his smoke and wondering where Sue has got to, when two men approach him and ask him for a match.

He gives them the box and then has a chance to look at them as they light their cigarettes. One of them is about 30, tough-looking with tidy, short hair. The other has long, straight hair and his denim jacket is covered in badges for Triumph and Status Quo. Ratface thinks they look a bit out of place here. He takes another drag on his spliff.

'Excuse me,' says the tough one expressionlessly, 'is that a marijuana cigarette you're smoking?'

Well, he can hardly deny it! The whole room must reek of the stuff by now. But he suddenly feels frightened as he says, 'Yes, maybe?'

The tough one puts his hand into his pocket and flashes a card at him. 'You're under arrest,' he says.

A shot of panic thuds into Ratty's heart. He checks the couple for a hint of a smile, but they remain stony-faced.

Ratface has imagined lots of things about dope in the past. Lots of times he's heard knocks on the door and imagined it must be the police. But he's never imagined this moment before, and he feels disgusted for letting himself be caught so easily. Of *course* I shouldn't have lit up here! Of *course* I should've known those bastards for what they are – bloody plain-clothes men! He looks at the longhair and thinks, How obvious! No one looks like that these days except a bloody policeman.

Damn, damn, maybe the bloody doorman tipped them off. I should've known something was funny when he put away those joints instead of lighting them up on the spot.

He's so keyed-up that he doesn't even notice that the lights have been fading. Now his heart misses another beat as the massed sounds of You and Your Bright Ideas! crash out over the speakers.

Then he thinks: Should I make a run for it? Should I start a riot? Where are the handcuffs? He looks down at his joint and wonders whether to throw it away, but it seems a bit of a waste . . . What the fuck's going on anyway?

He looks up at the hard-faced one and doesn't know what to say. Is he waiting for me to say something incriminating? Pass the smoke onto someone so they can nail them too?

'Had you fooled then, didn't we,' the man in the denims says without a smile.

Ratface feels even more stupid and ashamed than before. 'You bastards, you could've fucking given me a heart attack saying things like that. There are some things you just don't make jokes about.'

'I've been through it all before, mate,' says the one with short hair. 'I stick to the booze these days. Come on,' and he leads his friend off in the direction of the bar.

Ratface's heart is still beating fast as he takes the last few drags on the joint. Most unrelaxing smoke that turned out to be. Then his legs start feeling weary, and he pushes his way through the crowd to find a chair at the back. He sits down and nurses his head for a while; lets his nerves calm down.

Of course he can't see the band any more above all the haircuts, but that's immaterial. They're a rough-looking bunch anyway, and their music's jangling and harsh and unmelodic. I must say this, er, challenges one's preconceptions about music. . . but Ratface would sooner be listening to the thoughts inside his own head. He tries shutting his eyes for half a minute, but this only makes the music more penetrating and intolerable.

When he looks up again he notices a bunch of three lads, about 20 years old, standing to his right. They're shifting from foot to foot and spending most of their time hiding their faces behind their pint mugs. None of them is speaking, in fact they all look completely vacant. All three of them, Ratface notices with horror, are wearing shapeless flared corduroys. Two of them are wearing quilted anoraks, while the other is wearing a threadbare tweed jacket which reaches down almost to his knees. Ratface, who's always fancied himself as a bit of a physiognomist, begins staring at these specimens' faces.

A sorry lot indeed. The two in anoraks are presumably brothers, both have long untidy Prince Charles haircuts and large noses. He can see that their eyes are too close together, and deduces that they must be the children of a military man. The other character has a page-boy haircut which frames his stupid childish face. He's got a double chin, and quite a paunch too – not surprising considering the amount of beer he's knocking back.

But what really alarms Ratface, what really keeps his eyes transfixed, is that the one closest to him – with the anorak and the matted eyebrows and heavy nose – looks . . . well, there's just a shadow of a resemblance between this bloke and Ratface himself in his younger days.

Shameful. But true.

He's tried to forget the days, before he discovered dope, when he wore his hair greasy and parted down the left like a Tory MP. When he thought it was the height of chic to wear flared trousers, even if they were flapping three inches above his ankles. Now he finds himself observing a similar creature with unmitigated disgust.

I wonder if people looked at *me* with such contempt, he thinks. And then an even worse thought – Suppose I haven't actually changed at all! If I'm still as awkward and unattractive as I was then! He looks a bit tougher these days, a bit more streetwise, but he knows it's just a sham. He still hasn't recovered from the joke played on him earlier, that shows how 'streetwise' he is.

Ratface wonders whether to have another joint: will it calm his nerves or make him even more paranoid? Maybe that's what he gets off on after all, the 'paranoia hit'. The music is still as cacophonous and droning as before – another joint might enable him to appreciate it more.

He starts to weigh up the pros and cons, which is always a futile exercise because inevitably the more he thinks about it, the more he craves it. Such self-questionings always come down to, 'Well, I feel like one, so why not?' But this time his thought-process is interrupted by Sue suddenly appearing and sitting down next to him.

'I couldn't see you.' She has to shout to make herself heard above the music. 'Thought you must've gone.'

'I felt like it,' Ratface confesses. 'I'm not enjoying this much.'

> The Tory Government has decreed
> A metric week is what we need
> Your days are going to be deflated
> Your sleeping hours investigated.

Sue wonders, is this their new style, or are they all stoned? It sounds like ragtime heavy metal.

The people in the crowd don't want to dance. A few of them are swaying a little or tapping their toes awkwardly.

'What's wrong with you?' Linda shouts at the end of the fourth or fifth number. 'You all wearing Wrought Iron boots?'

Someone at the front yells back at them. Linda is incensed. 'What was that? "Get 'em off"? That's a typical male comment. Moronic and stupid. That's 'cos you're afraid of women, threatened by women in bands, you want to degrade us by telling us to undress!'

'I didn't say get 'em off!' The voice in the crowd is clearer this time. 'I said GET OFF! You're crap, the lot of you!'

Now Linda looks crushed. She turns despairingly to the drummer, who responds with a frenzied attack on his drumkit.

'That's no answer,' Ratface calls to Sue as the other instruments join in.

Sue shakes her head. Linda's always complaining that there's no money to be made in a band, but who wants to pay for such an assault on the eardrums. 'It's just a loud, painful noise to me. You might as well go and live next to Heathrow Airport.'

'We might as well do what?' shouts Ratface, eager for an alternative plan.

After the next song, Linda announces: 'I dedicate this song

to politicians and murderers everywhere!'

Ah, this must be their single. Sue can follow the words now.

The pinch of the recession must be felt
If you're starving just tighten your belt
Legless cripples stand up for yourselves.

NEEEEEEEE! The feedback coming through the speakers is quite deafening. Maybe the sound-man hogged the spliff for too long.

At last they decide to leave. Their ears are still ringing as they step out onto the street, and they have to carry on shouting.

Ratface says, 'Perhaps it was just an off-night.'

'They're a bit untogether, aren't they?' says Sue. 'But you can't knock 'em. They're always doing benefit gigs – they're playing at the "Keeping the Peace" gig next month, Rock against the Bomb . . . And look, their new single, they put it out themselves, they're completely independent. They've really stuck to their original ideals.'

Ratface examines the record. 'Mmm. Very sound. Shame we haven't got a turntable to play it on.'

# *Friday*

## *The proper channels*

Ratface is drawing on the wall opposite the cooker when Sue comes in with the evening paper. 'I'm sorry', he mumbles, 'I'll rub it out if you want, I just thought it looked a little bare and I got carried away.'

'Eh? What're you drawing, a little bear?'

'No. Well, I could do. Maybe I will.'

'What're you talking about? I thought that's what you said you were drawing. What's this creature here?'

'That's a badger. This is a fieldmouse, this is a sheep . . .'

'Yeah, I can see that.' She sits down to read her newspaper.

Ratface isn't sure whether to carry on or rub out the whole lot, so instead he starts reading over her shoulder. 'Eh, "Red Ken's Men in Junket Row", what's that, like Skid Row for junkies?'

'Oh, don't even look at it, it's all crap. This whole newspaper's crap, I only get it for the jobs.' And she turns to the Situations Vacant pages at the back.

'Hey, did you hear the thunderstorm last night? I've never heard anything like it in my life.'

'Yeah, it woke me up.'

'It woke me up too. I thought the lightning was going to hit the house for sure. I thought it was the end of the world.'

'Well, the paper-seller said he thought it was an omen, you know, a warning of doom to all the world leaders. I'm not supersititious like that. I reckon it was because of all the nuclear tests they keep on doing, fucking up the atmosphere.'

'Yeah. Hey, did you hear about the –'

'Oi, why don't you be quiet for a minute, I'm reading.'

'Can I have the news pages then?'

'I told you, there's no news in this paper.'

Ratface turns his attention to the radio, but a second later – 'Oh shit! I left it on all night! Damn, I turned it down when my mum came, now the batteries are flat . . .' Sue doesn't say anything, so he goes back to his drawing.

About 20 minutes later Sue bangs her fist on the table and exclaims: 'Crap! Crap! How can they print such crap!'

'Eh? What?' Ratface spins round.

'God, this is unbelievable. There's an article about the Greenham Common peace camp. This bloke says, "For me, the CND symbol is interchangeable with the swastika.' He must be mad. Look at this. He says, "The women whimper on about Life On Earth, but most of them are strident lesbians who can't produce Life On Earth anyway." Have you ever heard such bollocks?'

'Yeah, all the time in fact. Whad'you expect? Hey, let's have the jobs pages if you've finished with them.'

'There's no jobs in this paper. Hey, have you got a pen? I'm going to write to them. They can't get away with this . . . What shall I say? "I used to be a regular reader of your journal but now you have just gone too far." No, hang on . . . how about . . .' She jots down a few sentences, crosses them out and stares into space. 'No, what's the point of writing to them anyway? I know – I'll report them to the Press Council. I'll write to the Press Council. That should do it, I can't let them get away with this.'

As she writes, Ratface takes the newspaper and starts scanning it for jobs. 'Hey, what about this,' he says after a few minutes. 'This ad here, "I'm 23, I have my own yacht and two cars, last week I earned £1,000. If you want to be like me . . ." Sounds alright, why don't you go f'rit?'

'Eh, dunno, they always sound too good to be true. Why don't *you* go f'rit then?'

'Me? 'Cos what would I do with a yacht, two cars and a thousand quid a week? I don't want all that junk . . .'

'Oi, I do! What's he got again? Mmm. A thousand quid a week, eh. That's ridiculous! Just think of all the things you could do with a grand a week!'

'He probably slogs his guts out for it . . .'

'Alright then. But I wouldn't need as much as a thousand a week. Five hundred would do me fine. Or even three hundred, or even two . . . In fact I'd be happy with just a hundred, I could probably take it easy for a hundred a week, at that rate. If he can earn a hundred in . . . in an afternoon, then I could probably do it in two or three days a week . . . Yeah, sounds alright dunnit? I'll give it a go.' She finishes her letter and signs it with a triumphant flourish. 'Right, I'm going out to the Post Office to post this. I'll ring up this geezer too, let's see . . . "If you want to be like me, call Artie on 235 . . ." ' She writes down the number. 'God, Artie, I hate him already. But if he's offering me megabucks . . .'

'Artie. He must be a prat to advertise in the *News*,' says Ratface, turning over the page. 'Why d'you get this cruddy newspaper anyway?'

'Well. It's like Mrs Thatcher keeps on saying . . . Tina.'

'Eh? Tina?'

'Yeah – there is no alternative, see?'

# *Legal highs*

Shit, twenty past eight, I'm late enough – how dare Peter be late too? He should be waiting for me. What else has he got to do with his time? I could go for a walk I suppose, but – oh hell, 'Half o' lager ta.'

Fancy being stood up by Peter Hewlett! After all this time. Banana-legs, that's what they used to call him at school, because of the way he walked. I never had a nickname at school thank God, I was always just Dan or Danny Boy; but some of the other kids got lumbered with some horrendous names, Sponge, that's right, and Skinny Dick and Nappies. Where are they all now? Blithering wrecks, maybe, psychiatric cases still traumatised by the weight of accumulated insult. Not that *I* was the worst, not compared with some of those fledgling fascists, but sometimes, well, there was Bonehead and Quasimodo, sometimes it *was* funny!

Lager's crap. Should've brought a newspaper to read, it's boring looking at the wallpaper and the light fittings and the bottom of my glass. Peter, Peter, what the fuck's happened to you?

The Old Lion is filling up now. It's Friday night and soon there'll be no room to move, let alone sit down. A party of well-dressed young professional types comes and poses near where he's sitting. Now, there's even fewer places to look, I wouldn't want anyone to think I'm staring at *them*!

'Excuse me, is anyone sitting here?'

'Yes, my friend's sitting there.' You didn't think I had any friends, did you, you poser? Not everyone hates me, you know, I don't normally have to resort to boozing on my own.

At this moment Pete walks in, gives a perfunctory glance around the pub and homes in on Dan's table. 'Sorry I'm late,' he says coolly. 'Can I get you another drink?'

'Maybe another half of lager. Thanks.'

So Pete marches off to the bar and returns in under a minute with the half-pint and a double whisky.

'What kept you?' Dan says as Pete sits down. 'I've been here for ages.'

'I'm terribly sorry, I popped into the wine-bar after work, obligations, you know how it is . . . Actually I had a quick drink with Caroline Tucker, do you remember Caroline?'

Caroline? Yes, of course Dan remembers Caroline. The most sought-after girl in the whole school, God, a whole host of people made fools of themselves over Caroline. 'Yeah, 'course. How come you're still seeing *her*?'

'She's working at Craig Belafonte. In personnel. She's been with us for six months, so I see quite a lot of her – go and see films, plays . . . that sort of thing.'

Don studies Pete's face carefully. He doesn't mean . . . they're sleeping together? Banana-legs having an affair with Caroline Tucker, no, he can't believe it. Sneaky sod. Probably Caroline can't even remember what Banana-legs was like at school, otherwise she'd never be considering going out with him now.

'So what's this job you've got at – Craig . . .'

'Craig Belafonte. They're a multinational company involved in market research in Britain, the States, France . . . I work in promotions. It's a fascinating job, there's lots of travelling and I get to meet lots of people. They've given me a company car and soon I'll be taking out clients to lunch, all on expenses! Not bad, eh?'

'How much are you getting?'

'Hmm . . . after tax . . . let's say I'm comfortable. Pretty comfortable.' A Rod Stewart song is droning away on the jukebox. 'How about you, what are you doing at the moment?'

'Not a lot. I just lost my job a couple of days ago, so I'm on the dole now.'

'You got made redundant? That's terrible. Oh dear. What were you doing?'

'Wasn't doing nothing, I just got the sack! Oh sorry – I was working in a theatre booking agency in the West End. Business falling off, they said, so they gave me the chop. As if that was my fault! I can't help it if they don't know how to run a bloody booking agency.'

'Oh dear. So I suppose now you're hunting around for another job.'

'Yeah. I suppose. You know, I reckon I've missed the boat now. When I left school it was so easy to get work, casual work, that kind of thing. Now there's nothing. I don't know if I'll ever get another job.'

'No, I'm sure you'll find something. I don't think we've got any vacancies at Craig Belafonte at the moment, but . . .'

Well I can do without your patronage thank you! Dan shrugs his shoulders.

'I'd better get you another drink,' Pete says. 'Same again, or do you want a pint this time?'

'Oh no, hold on, it's my round. . .'

But Pete is already on his feet. 'No, I'll buy them, you can't afford it if you're unemployed.' Dan wonders whether to be offended by this, but Pete continues: 'You can do the same for me if you find a job and I lose mine.'

'Yeah – huh! No one's safe these days. You'd better watch out, you never know who's next in line for the chop.'

While Pete's waiting at the bar, Dan takes another look at the people around him. The trendy socialites have pissed off – to a party probably – but the pub's getting fuller all the time. Nearby, three lads are sitting sprawled around a table; they're talking so loud that Dan doesn't have to strain much to overhear them. They're grimacing grotesquely and banging their fists and yelling Faahking this and Faahking that. One of them slaps another on the back, and the third exclaims, 'Oi! I saw that! Sometimes I worry about you two.' 'Eh? Whaddaya mean?' 'I saw you touch him, sometimes I wonder about you two.' 'Urgh, faahking L. Bleeeuch. Could you go for that, eh?' 'No, faahking L, could you go for that eh?' 'Bleeeuch. No, I couldn't go for that. Imagine that, a shaft up your bum.' 'Bleeeuch. Could you go for that?' 'No, if someone tried to stick their shaft up my bum I'd fucking kill 'em.' 'Makes you sick, I'd kill the lot of 'em.' 'Fucken shafts up each others' bums. No, me, I worry about you two. Bleeeuch, could you go for that then, eh?'

The jukebox is turned up as Peter returns with the drinks. They have to shout to make themselves heard above the twittering of Assorted Pleasures.

> We're living in a big balloon
> The silver lining's coming soon
> Take my hand we'll go together
> Through the dark and stormy weather.

Now Dan thinks of a few things to say, a few things to ask, but it takes too much effort to speak above the din. He just says, 'This music's crap, isn't it?' and Pete replies: 'I don't know, d'you like them?' Again Dan doesn't know what to say, no no I said it's crap – but it's not worth explaining.

At last he says, 'We've got to move further from the jukebox. Look, those two over there are just leaving.' A middle-aged couple by the door are gathering up their possessions. So Dan and Pete make a bee-line for their seats and glide into them before anyone else has a chance.

The music isn't so deafening here, but still most of the people are sitting in silence, interested only in their alcohol. Dan gets a coughing fit because a stream of smoke from someone's cigarette is heading inescapably up his nostrils.

Pete announces he's going to the Gents. A gentle, weepy number comes on the jukebox, soothing Dan's ears; and now he becomes aware of another sound, a strange croaking noise, like a frog drowning in someone's beer. It's not his stomach rumbling, it's too regular. There must be an undercover policeman sitting nearby, it's his radio . . . But again, no, none of these geriatrics and no-hopers could possibly be an undercover cop.

Eventually he traces the noise to the video-game machine a few yards away. Maybe some insect, a cricket or something, is sitting behind it . . . but as he approaches it, he realises the sound is neither human nor animal. It's a voice, but it's coming from inside the machine. It's saying monotonously: 'Insert – Coin. Insert – Coin. Insert – Coin.'

Dan's irritated at having been deceived. No, fucked if I'm going to insert a coin into your ravenous little belly! You parasite, you're never sated are you. It's not even 'Please insert coin' – you're giving orders! Well, I'm not playing. You can cry as much as you like, you're not swallowing my money. 'Insert – Coin. Insert – Coin.' These bloody Japanese inventions . . . Do all the Japanese obey orders, Dan wonders as he sits down. I can just imagine them queuing up compliantly, like robots, waiting to insert their coins . . . though I mustn't be racist. Most English people are pretty much like robots too, especially in pubs. If you could programme a robot to sit and drink in a pub, well, probably no one would notice the difference.

And Pete – has he become a robot too? Dan watches him as he returns from the bog. He's carrying another round of drinks. 'Oh no, you shouldn't've done that, it was my turn' – but Pete shrugs him off.

'Anyway, I mustn't drink any more after this,' Dan goes on. 'I'm on my motorbike, so two pints is my limit.'

'Two pints? Christ, two pints of whisky is *my* limit! I can always drive. I don't give a shit for the legal limit.'

'No, but I do! . . . *You* go on drinking 'cos if you have an accident you'll be alright – just a dent or two in your car, that's all. But what if you hit a pedestrian? What if you hit a biker? You could fucking kill someone. That's not bloody funny.'

'Well, I can take my alcohol,' Pete says proudly. 'I've got a good head.'

A good head! You mean you have shit for brains more like.

There's nothing in your head, if you're going to drive around loaded. Please, when we leave, give me a ten-minute start so that I can get well clear of you! He says, 'I don't drink hardly at all these days, in fact. It's not safe. Anyway it's so bloody expensive, and it just goes in tax . . .'

'Ah yes, tax,' Pete says. Pause. 'No one likes paying it but we've got to have it.'

'Yeah, but what does it go on, that's the question! Hospitals and schools and so on, that's one thing, but I don't want my money buying nuclear missiles.'

'Ah yes, nuclear missiles. No one likes them but we've got to have them.'

'What's that? Bollocks! Bollocks we've got to have them. Tell me, what possible use are they? To pay for them we're making people go hungry and sick and ignorant. And why do we need them?'

'We must have an independent deterrent . . . in case Russia decides to invade. We must be protected against the Russians. I know, CND and all that, but what would you actually do if the Soviets invaded?'

'Christ, what would the *Soviets* do if they decided to invade?! Sign on the dole? Why the fuck d'you think the Russians would want to come here – to take over our industry? We haven't got any industry! I reckon the Government's adopted a scorched earth policy!'

Pete says: 'Britain's in a very good position, strategically. The Russians would love to stockpile weapons here, and direct them on Europe and the States.'

'Well, no worries then. Now we're just waiting for them, aren't we – all they have to do is re-direct the existing weapons! And instead of *them* paying for the missiles, it's you and me who's paid for them, in our taxes. Great!'

Pete lights a cigar. 'Also you mustn't forget that the weapons industry provides a vast number of jobs. It's very important for our economy.'

'Phoo! That's not an argument! That's like saying we've got

to have mass unemployment otherwise all the dole-office staff would be made redundant.' Pete's looking at the barmaid, he doesn't seem to be listening. 'Look, how come the Russians are our enemy anyway? Answer me that. How come we have to drain the country dry because of them?'

'They threaten us – they threaten our way of life.' Pete says this conclusively as if he's a great authority on the subject. Oh yes, thank you, Professor Hewlett, for part four of your lecture on the British way of life – the smoky cancerous pubs with the resident bigot, the cold and the damp, death with the vicar and a royal event every summer. And what about freedom of speech? There's no freedom of speech in this dingy den, not if you're sitting too close to the jukebox.

'Anyway, Nostradamus says the Antichrist is going to come from the East. We've got to protect ourselves.'

Dan sips his beer. Nostradamus! Bet he never predicted the whole world would end up down the pub.

'Hey Danny – d'you remember Johnny Pratt at school? After he left he became a heroin addict apparently, and then he reformed and joined the Hare Krishnas.'

'No . . . I don't remember . . .' Smack addict, probably smoked a bit of dope that's all! Always divide rumours by ten.

'Can I get you another drink?'

'No, no, definitely not. Thanks. I've had my limit.'

'Are you sure? D'you mind if I get myself one then? Mustn't run the risk of getting thirsty on the way home.'

'Go ahead!'

Pete gets up and Dan looks around the room again. The men who don't want shafts up their bums are preparing to leave and grimacing as they go. At another table a well-dressed man is lying on his face in front of two full pints of beer; he could be dead for all anyone cares. And over there two nervous young women have been accosted by a bloke in a suit, the bloke's laughing heartily and treading on everyone's toes. Never give up do you, Pete.

Go on, you can get yourself a drink. You can get them a

drink too if you want. You tried to impress me and I tried to impress you and now you can try to impress them. It's getting late and I don't want to wait around for the inevitable mass rendition of 'My Way' at closing-time. We can carry on our conversation just as meaningfully by ourselves. Good luck then. And goodbye.

# *A midnight run*

Dan comes into the kitchen and sees Ratface rolling a joint. 'Oh, stoke that one up!' he says eagerly. 'My nerves need calming down.'

'Where've you been?' asks Sue. 'I've been waiting for you. You're so late.'

'Thanks, why this sudden concern about my welfare? I just had a couple of drinks with an old mate – not much of a mate, in fact.'

'So why d'you need calming down if you've been drinking all evening?'

'This bloke was really winding me up, that's why. What a wally! Anyway I haven't been drinking all evening, I had a couple that's all. Come on, I haven't had a smoke all day!'

Ratface gives him the joint to light up. Dan tokes at it gingerly, just wanting to be soothed a little, not to be pole-axed across the skull. As he passes it to Sue he notices the drawing opposite the stove. 'God, Diane's kids haven't been round here again have they? They've been scribbling on the walls.' Ratface looks embarrassed.

'Never mind about that,' says Sue. 'Take a look at this.' She passes Dan the newspaper and points at the headline: THE KREMLIN'S STOOGES.

He reads the article perfunctorily. 'Why d'you want me to read that? It's complete bollocks.'

'I know it's bollocks. You think *you* were wound up! I wrote to the Press Council when I saw that, I had to, I was so furious . . .'

'Yeah? Good – writing to the Press Council. Mind you, it's just pissing in the wind, it's all the establishment.'

'I know it's all the establishment. That's why I had another idea. That's why I've been waiting for you. That's why I bought this.' And she shows Dan a can of spraypaint. "I reckon this is the best way of getting my views across. I can write even bigger than a *News* headline! I want to write for everyone to read, know what I mean? Not just the Press Council. I'm going to write it in big green letters on the *Evening News* headquarters.'

'Green's original,' says Dan.

'Well, I couldn't get black or white because the building might be black or white. And I didn't want to get red because they'd think I'm a communist, and I'm not a communist, I'm a woman.'

'So where do I come into it? Why were you waiting for me?'

'Because I'm not going to do the deed and then wait for a bloody bus! I want to borrow your bike.'

'Borrow my bike! You must be crazy. Have you got a licence? You'd probably get arrested, or crash . . . I didn't even know you could ride a bike.'

'Necessity is the mother of invention . . .'

'Eh? No, you must be crazy! You're not . . .'

'Hey! Only joking. Course I can ride a bike. Think only big, tough men can ride, eh?'

'Well you *can't* ride – you're not riding my bike. Not at this time of night, not until you've proved you're competent. Not for some crackpot scheme.'

'What d'you mean, crackpot scheme? What's crackpot about it? I thought you were in favour of a bit of free expression.'

'Yeah, yeah . . .'

'I mean, everyone's entitled to put forward an opinion, and if you don't own a newspaper you just have to improvise.'

'Mm. Alright.'

'Alright what?'

'Alright, I'll take you.'

'I don't want to be taken! I want to go there myself. If you're afraid of being caught – I don't want to go with someone who's afraid of being caught.'

'Alright, I'm not afraid. Not as afraid as if I let *you* ride. Come on, I'll take you or we're both staying here.'

So Sue gives in. 'There'll be no interference from you, mind. You'll let me do what I want to do. I'll write what I want to write. And when I say ride, you'll ride like the clappers.'

The journey to central London is a smooth and easy one. The maniac car drivers must be at home now, sleeping off the evening's excesses. Luckily there's not a hint of rain. And Sue's a safe passenger, she sits well forward and moves with the bike: unlike most of Dan's male friends, who sit far back to avoid any body contact and who consequently are able to steer the machine like a rudder.

The *Evening News* office is in Turnpike Lane, which turns out to be a small alley tucked away from the main road. They get off the bike, but they leave their helmets on as they survey the building.

'It's a bit of a hole,' says Sue, disappointed. 'No one's even going to notice if I spray something here.'

'Well, 'snot Piccadilly Circus. But if you want to protest against the *Evening News* . . . What're you going to write anyway? Better make it quick.'

Sue shakes the can of spraypaint and says: 'I'm not sure. I want to say – "Look out you fascists because women are angry." '

'It's a bit long, isn't it? This is a dead-end street, we'll be trapped like spiders in a bath if a police car comes by while you're spraying.'

'I thought I told you no interference,' Sue retorts. 'I can't make it much shorter than that, not unless I write "The Clash" or "Kilroy was Here".'

'Well get on with it then. I don't want to be nicked.' He looks around to make sure that no one is coming.

'Coward,' says Sue, and chooses a space on the wall where her slogan will fit.

'Aw, cut the flourishes, what're you planning, a bloody illuminated manuscript?'

'I warned you!' Sue squeezes the nozzle tentatively, but there's just a splutter and no paint comes out. She examines the instructions on the can – 'Shake for at least two minutes before use'. So she gives it another long, vigorous shake, and the ball-bearing inside rattles like a castanet. Shit, she thinks, I bet they make it deliberately noisy so that graffiti artists can't function in peace – I sound like a bloody steel band about to start up!

Dan's still looking nervously up and down the street and at the office windows. Suddenly he hisses: 'Quick! Put it away! Someone's coming!' He rushes over to the bike and kick-starts it.

Sue clambers onto the back, saying: 'What's the matter? If it's a false alarm – ' But she doesn't complete her threat. Turning round, she sees a light has gone on in the office hallway, she sees the door being pushed open by a man in uniform . . .

'Sit straight!' Dan yells sharply, and whizzes out of the alley and onto the main road with a great roar of engines.

'Hey! Look where you're going then! There could've been something coming the other way!'

Dan ignores her, but a few moments later he slows down and shouts to Sue again: 'Did you write anything? Did they see us?'

'No, the bloody spray didn't work, did it. Someone came out – out of the building, I mean. I don't know if they saw us, you told me to turn round.'

Dan thinks: What if they've got a radio, what if they took down my number? They could've rung the police. We have to get out of here. So he turns off onto a side road and is able to relax a little.

The bike's brought to a standstill by a set of red lights. As they're waiting, a police car pulls up behind them. Now Dan's heart starts to thump. Yes, thank Christ his headlight's on. I hope the back light's working. I hope I don't stall . . . The lights turn green and Dan expects the police car to surge forward, lights flashing, and stop them. Bring the whole weight of the law down on them with a dreadful thud. But the police car turns left and vanishes out of view.

His heart continues to thump as he rides on. He thinks: If only I hand't had those two pints tonight, if only I'd stuck to the dope! You can't smell dope on the breath, and it makes you calmer too. Many's the time he's been stopped by the police, stoned out of his gourd, and been able to say yes-officer, no-officer and coolly bluff his way out. But if he's stopped now – they'll smell he's been drinking and cart him off. Dan breathes in and out quickly a few times to try to freshen his mouth, but instead it just makes his scarf reek of stale beer.

Sue yells again – 'Where are you going? Remember I haven't sprayed anything yet!'

'I'm not going back there! They'll be waiting for us.'

They're now approaching Charing Cross. 'Let's go to Buckingham Palace,' says Sue.

'You mad? It's swarming with police since the break-in!' But he drives through Admiralty Arch and stops the bike just beyond it. The Palace is visible half a mile away up the Mall. 'Is this any good? I'm not going any closer.'

Sue sighs but dismounts and looks around for a likely spot. There are no walls, so she'll have to write something on the road. Well, that's a prominent enough place, and who knows – maybe the Queen will read her message as she swishes by in her Limousine. 'What can I write here? "Jobs not Bombs"? That's a cliché . . . How about "Women Rule"?'

'We know that already.'

'Ah, *I* know . . .'

The street is poorly lit, but Sue can see that it's completely deserted. Dan rides his bike into the shadows of St James's Park and waits there, keeping the engine running. Sue shakes the aerosol and starts to write – WOM.

'Quick!' calls Dan, and Sue darts onto the curb as a car

appears from the Arch. It zooms harmlessly by, and she carries on – WOMEN SA.

Dan shouts out again, this time a car is coming the other way, from the Palace. Sue rushes over to where he's waiting. 'They'll see it for sure,' he says, watching the headlights as they come closer. As the car draws level, the words glisten and shine as if Sue's using luminous paint. 'Well, it's not a police car but you can never be sure. Get a move on.'

Sue's horrified when she steps out and surveys her handiwork. 'It's all ruined! The wankers! They've smeared it all, it looks like someone's had a do-it-yourself lobotomy!'

'Come back!' Dan yells – another car is coming from the direction of the Palace.

She joins him and says: 'It's useless, you can't read it now. Can't we find a nice quiet wall somewhere?'

'What! How much more d'you want to write?'

'I still haven't written anything. It's completely illegible, so you needn't worry – the police'll never know there's a graffiti artist on the loose.'

She gets on the pillion and Dan checks the coast is clear before riding off. 'You're right,' he says, examining the mess. 'It looks like King Kong threw up.' He slows down as they enter Trafalgar Square. 'Where to now?'

'Let's go to Parliament.'

So they ride down Whitehall to Westminster, but everything's too brightly lit. Police are patrolling the area, and there are even some late-night sightseers. Dan turns left by the Houses of Parliament, and finds the Embankment surprisingly quiet and dimly lit.

A row of grandiose office buildings is set back a little way from the road. In the daytime they'll be swarming with civil servants and tourists, but at the moment there's not a soul around. Over the river, on County Hall, a huge sign declares: LONDON'S JOBLESS – 357,432.

Dan parks the bike in a deserted gateway and says: 'The Ministry of Defence is near here, isn't it? Let's leave the bike here, no one can see it from the road. Hey, have you got any identification on you, anything with your name on it?'

'No, why?'

'Good. Then even if we're caught they won't be able to trace us. Let's leave our helmets here too, so they won't trace the bike. We can pretend we're Scandinavian tourists, lovers taking a stroll . . .'

'Or good friends taking a stroll,' Sue corrects him. Dan locks up the helmets, and they set off towards the ministry buildings.

Sue says: 'You'd better drive a bit more carefully on the way home. Christ, when you drove off from the *Evening News* office – I thought I was going to fly off the back!'

'Better than getting caught, isn't it?'

'And then going round those corners, I wanted to *jump* off the back! You were going much too fast, it's so dangerous . . . Hey, what's this building? Why are we here?'

'The Ministry of Defence is around here,' Dan repeats. They walk on, through a little shady park separating the offices from the road. 'I don't know where . . . it's not this place.'

Sue groans and Dan tries to change the subject. 'What were you trying to spray down the Mall? "Women say" something.'

'Women say disarm or die,' says Sue.

'Hmm. Yeah, like it. But why not just say "Disarm or die"? I mean, men say it too.'

'Men start wars. Men like wars.'

'No, only generals and psychopaths like war. Men get killed in wars, most of them don't have any choice. Ninety-nine per cent of men don't gain anything from war.'

'At least men get glory. This culture thinks it's glorious to be killed in battle.'

'Glory! What's glory? A Union Jack over your dead body . . . We should go out and spray something on the Cenotaph, "The Grateful Dead", it makes about as much sense as "The Glorious Dead". What's glorious about being dead?'

'Men like wars,' Sue persists. 'They like fighting and looting and raping, and it'll go on till *women* put a stop to it. Take away your weapons. Fuck it – where are we going? Have you got a clue? Why did you leave the bike so far away?'

'I didn't want to take it onto the pavement . . . I thought the Ministry of Defence was here . . .'

'Well it's not, is it. Whose bright idea was it to come here in the first place? I warned you about no interference. And now you're telling me you don't like my slogan! Always have to interfere, don't you. Well, you can think up your own slogan if you're so clever!' And she thrusts the can of spraypaint into Dan's hand and strides off.

'Hey! What's this! Where are you going?' But she doesn't even turn round. Oh shit, I've done it now. Me and my big mouth!

There's no point arguing with her, anyway they'd wake all the night watchmen within miles. What's he to do now?

His first idea is to dump the can and return to the bike. But, well, he doesn't want to waste the journey or the paint. And the Ministry of Defence should be somewhere nearby . . . He hides the can in his jacket and walks on. Past the side turning which Sue took – what's she going to do, take a taxi home? Maybe not such a bad idea, Dan feels a real amateur using a Honda 175 as a getaway vehicle.

A couple of people walk by; can't do anything here anyway, it's a bit open. Dan turns and sees a huge mock-classical building with doors which look as if they belong to the strong-room at Fort Knox. This is it, he recognises it. Yes of course it's here, what was I thinking of?

He's surprised to find no guards, no sign of life, not even any lurking IRA terrorists. Just a little plaque saying 'Ministry of Defence'. He wonders what he should write, and where. There's no one around at the moment, but a police car could appear at any second and there would be no escape, nowhere to hide.

What was Sue's slogan? . . . No, she said make up one of your own. What about 'Money for life not death' – a bit long. 'No Cruise', that's a bit weak . . . I must carry on walking, I mustn't look suspicious! He walks past the entrance three times, trying to think of a pithy slogan. At last he runs up the steps, checks that no one's coming, rattles the can and sprays the word DEATH in foot-high letters on the plaque, so that it reads 'Ministry of Death'.

It's not very dramatic, but as he puts down the can and scurries away his heart is racing again. He's wearing his bike-gloves, so there won't be any fingerprints on the can . . . are there any paint-specks on his clothes? Now he must stop running, he mustn't draw attention to himself. He looks round at the bright green letters and thinks, maybe red *would* have been better. It's really not very impressive – but it's still more than my nerves can take!

As he's nearing the junction, he hears a car engine behind him and instinctively turns round. His face flushes and his whole body breaks out in a sweat when he sees a police car coming towards him. He feels that his face must be like a beacon, glowing with guilt in the dark. He tells himself to keep on walking and be calm, but he's even finding it difficult to walk, his legs give way and he staggers a little. His path isn't straight either, he concentrates on keeping it straight but now his feet feel like bricks and he has to drag them along. He turns the junction with a huge sense of relief. He tries to remain casual and look straight ahead, but soon the tension rises in him again. What's happened to the policemen? Are they examining the graffitti? Or are they following me, observing me in silence, taking note of my guilt-ridden clumsiness? About to leap out and grab me?

I'm a Scandinavian tourist, that's all I am. Svensk. I never saw anything! At last the tension reaches such an unbearable pitch that he can't refrain from looking behind him. The police car has disappeared.

Now Dan feels drained, he feels stupid for having got so worked up. The police didn't even notice my pissing little word. Five little letters – Sue's going to think it's pathetic when I tell her! Not exactly going to make anyone stop and think, is it? I might as well have written 'Duran Duran' in the toilets at Victoria Station. And there was me shitting myself . . . That police car probably took two years off my life just now, they saved the judge the trouble!

As he approaches his motorbike, he suddenly realises he's missing something – his helmet! No, of course, he left them in the helmet-lock; but when he looks, there's nothing there.

Now he starts to feel sick. Did Sue come and take them? No, that's ridiculous, she wouldn't do a think like that, anyway she went the other way. But then who did take them? You don't expect helmet thieves to be roaming round the Embankment at one-thirty in the morning. Why weren't the police doing their job, eh? Or maybe it's a police trap! Well, I'm not going to fall for it, I'm not going to be lured into any police station. And I'm not going to hang around here looking for clues, either; I'm getting out of here right away. He looks up at the sky and says: 'Get me out of this, yeah?'

Of course it's against the law to ride a motorbike without a helmet, unless you're a Sikh and your religion dictates that you must wear a turban. But Dan hasn't enough money for a taxi; suddenly he's feeling crushingly tired and he longs for his bed. So he doesn't have much choice. He'll have to become a Sikh for the night.

He finds his handkerchief in the recesses of his pocket, ties a knot in each corner, and puts it on his head. It's quite dirty, but what's a bit of snot in your hair? It's better than walking home or going to the police or joining the tramps under the bridge.

He starts up the engine, makes sure that no one's in sight, and then roars off northwards. Only one car passes him on the Embankment, a little blue sports car which flashes past swerving erratically. The driver's probably too plastered to notice.

Dan quickly plans a route which will take him home through some secluded backstreets. He zig-zags his way through the quiet streets, bursting with anticipation, praying that he won't be caught. Around Tottenham Court Road he runs into a network of one-way streets and finds himself going round in a circle. He's expecting to run into a patrol car around every corner, but still no one comes.

His head felt a bit light before, but now – buffeted by the night air – it seems to be disconnected from his body, and his body seems disconnected from his bike. It feels as if he's whizzing along suspended in mid-air, and he wonders what'll happen if he looks down – maybe he'll come crashing down to earth like Bugs Bunny when he runs over a cliff.

A few pedestrians look at him as he zooms by. What are they doing at this time of night anyway? Up to no good, no doubt.

He touches his head and finds the handkerchief still sitting there securely. Well, it's no more useless than the brain-bucket which Sue wears, the one she picked up for 50 pence at a jumble sale. Maybe from a distance, in the dark, a short-sighted person could mistake the grey–white rag for an old-fashioned helmet – the sort which Fag-Ash Joe wears as he puffs along on his little moped.

Brought to a halt by some traffic lights, he looks at his reflection in his mirror. He's appalled by what he sees. His eyes stare guiltily back at him, his face is contorted by the cold and the knotted hanky looks completely ridiculous. No, it could hardly be mistaken for a helmet, or even a turban; he looks like a rapist trying to mingle on Brighton Beach.

The shock of seeing his own face makes him drive on still more recklessly. If anyone comes in sight, he accelerates even harder and wills himself to become invisible. If the police come now . . . they'll have a good laugh, for sure.

Rounding a bend, he has to clamp on his brakes when he sees a police van ahead of him. A policeman is questioning a car driver. Dan does a hasty U-turn and escapes down the nearest side turning. Keep him talking, mate, keep him talking!

He almost collides with a red Renault coming from his right. The car screeches to a halt but Dan carries on, even faster now, straining at the handlebars. He feels as if he's in a dream. The engine's not going to give up on him is it? And shit, the petrol tank's on reserve, it's been on reserve since yesterday and I've driven miles since then.

A bunch of lads see him and call out: 'Oi, you forgot your helmet!' Sssh, not so loud eh! Two cars pass in the opposite direction, and now a car behind him starts flashing its headlights. Yeah, yeah, I had noticed! He drives closer to the kerb to let the car pass. The driver toots his horn as he overtakes. Thanks a lot!

But the roads seem to be getting too busy around here – probably everyone going home from late-night parties. Dan's nearing home now anyway so he decides not to take any more risks. He can walk home from here. He parks the bike, locks it, and removes his headgear.

What a relief it is to be walking again – what a relief to be legal! He has a piss in somebody's flower-bed and lets his nerves calm down. I wonder what time it is? I wonder what happened to Sue? It's quite lucky she left when she did, because she could never have ridden on the back without a helmet. Killing yourself, that's your own business; but killing someone else is quite another matter.

And Sue was so angry – she'd've been even crosser if she'd stayed! 'You can't help interfering, can you?' that's what she said. Maybe I am a bossy sorty of person, maybe I'm just a sexist pig. What about that time the other day when she got cross at me for tidying away all her job applications? 'I can keep my own affairs in order, thank you very much.' I suppose I was interfering then as well.

Maybe I'm impatient. Maybe I'm obsessional. Maybe Sue really doesn't like me at all, thinks I'm a creep and a busybody and wants me to move out. The flat's not big enough for three people after all. I should ask her tomorrow, come straight out with it.

And earlier when she said – 'You think only men can ride bikes.' Perhaps I should've lent her the bike, it was selfish of me not to. She may not have a licence, but then I don't have a licence to ride around like a maniac with a knotted hanky on my head.

Dan begins to feel weak with guilt and shame. Will Sue be waiting for me in the kitchen, waiting to slag me off? I couldn't handle any more stress tonight, if she's there I'll have to try and creep in unnoticed . . .

But as he rounds the corner into Griggs Road and looks up at the flat he can see that all the lights are off. Sue's probably been in bed for ages. Dan tiptoes up the stairs and opens and closes the front door with a minimum of noise.

He goes into the kitchen and has a glass of water. Ratface's rolling equipment is on the table – papers, matches and a sprinkling of grass. Ratty won't mind if I have a little number . . . I deserve it after all I've been through. So he rolls one and goes into his bedroom to smoke it.

Halfway through the joint he begins to feel sick and dizzy so he puts it out and undresses and crawls into bed. Half a minute later the nausea subsides so he lights it again and finishes it off.

Now when he leans back and shuts his eyes, his head starts swinging so wildly that he thinks he's going to be sick. He forces open his eyes and focuses on the Maggie's Farm poster opposite his bed. His brain rocks to a halt.

When he starts drifting again, he's on his bike. Driving along a gloomy backstreet . . . easing round a corner . . . when suddenly WHAM! The red Renault has gone straight into him! His whole body jerks as if an electric current has passed through him, and his eyes spring open. Shit, he thinks, I drove like a madman tonight! I've got to be more careful, you can't take risks riding a bike in London. I could've been killed. In fact, I should've been killed. I was in such a blind panic when that car appeared . . . how come I *wasn't* killed?

It was so close . . . Maybe I was killed! Maybe the car did hit me, and I flew off the bike and smashed my head on the pavement. I'd never have known anything about it. How do I know that didn't happen? How do I know I haven't been imagining everything since then, because I haven't been able to come to terms with the shock of dying? Maybe I'm not really here at all . . . I've heard that kind of thing can happen. Someone will appear to me in the night and say 'Come on Daniel Kinnell, your time is up, you were killed tonight in a road accident, the police are clearing up the mess and your body's in the morgue.' But it'll be cold in the morgue, I don't want to leave my bed, I don't want to leave Ratty and Sue and Lesley and Jerry and Steve. I don't want to be taken away! If necessary I'll keep my eyes open all night, no one's going to come and take me away.

He finds his soft toy crocodile on the floor and puts it in his bed to cuddle. Well, maybe I can close my eyes, but I mustn't fall asleep. I must be watchful tonight. No one's going to come and take me away. No one. No one. No one.

# Saturday

## *Don't look back*

When Dan awakes he knows it's already late. So much for his resolution. Luckily he still seems to be alive. His stomach feels queasy when he tries to move and his head feels swollen and tender. He strokes Crocodile and thinks, I shouldn't've had that smoke last night, I shouldn't've had those two pints. He feels like lying as still as possible and groaning in peace, but he needs a leak and he can't hold on any longer. So he gets up, very carefully, puts on some clothes and goes to the bathroom.

When he comes out, he bumps into Sue. 'Hi, glad you got back alright!' she says. 'I went into your room earlier to check you were okay, but you were asleep.'

Suddenly Dan feels light-headed with relief. What, no recriminations? He follows her into the kitchen and says: 'Fuckin' L, what a time I had. I don't know how I made it back.' He gets himself a glass of water and sits down.

'Did you write anything, or did you just piss off home? Sorry I got angry . . . I freaked out a bit, that's all.'

'Yeah, well I found the Ministry of Defence at last. I changed the sign on it to read 'Ministry of Death'.'

'Really? Ministry of Death, yeah, that's quite good! How big did you write it? Did it show up?'

'The letters were . . . a couple of foot high maybe. It showed up but it wasn't blinding, know what I mean?' And it didn't really look like Ministry of Death, either, more like Ministry of Defence with Death scrawled over it. But just after I dumped the can a police car appeared, I thought they'd see it for sure! The paint still dripping wet . . . ' Dan smiles. He was walking like a rag-doll last night, the police were probably too busy laughing at him to notice a bit of fresh green graffiti.

'I was afraid you might've crashed. I couldn't see the bike outside, where'd you park it?'

'About a mile away in fact, I suppose I should go and pick it up. Shit, I'll have to use that crumby orange open-face helmet.'

'Why, what happened? Where are the helmets?'

'Got nicked, didn't they. Went back to the bike and someone'd cut right through the straps. I don't know who could've done it – some NF gits, some rugger-buggers maybe.'

'Shit. So what d'you do? Ha! Don't tell me you tried pushing the bike all the way home! Bloody good getaway vehicle it turned out to be! Lucky there wasn't anyone chasing you.'

'What d'you mean, did I push it? I'd've got arrested for sure. I rode it back.'

'What! Without a helmet! I think you're nuts.'

Yeah, but not as nuts as you'd think I was if you knew what I was wearing on my head for protection . . . 'I left it in Moss Street in the end, I didn't want to push my luck.'

'So you going to pick it up now?'

'I'd better.' He has another drink of water, and finds the orange helmet in the cupboard under the sink. 'I might go off for a hack after. It looks nice out.'

Half of London has also decided it's nice out. So they're sitting in their little metal boxes pumping noxious gases into the atmosphere. Dan watches them as they chug slowly up the street. He feels like shouting at them – Oi, you'll never find the sun in there! A heart attack more like.

He carries on over the railway bridge, past the two huge painted slogans which no one has ever bothered to erase: 'Ban Polaris' on one side and 'M. Khan is a Poof' on the other. He finds his bike standing where he left it. Alright, fancy a little burn then? I deserve to enjoy myself on my first Saturday of freedom.

Waiting at the lights on Petley Road he catches sight of his reflection in some shop doors to his right. How strange, he thinks, it looks like I'm carrying someone on the pillion! Of course it must be an illusion, the reflection of a passer-by . . . but when he turns to his left there are no passers-by. He looks at the shop again – there's still someone behind me! Did someone jump on or am I taking the devil for a ride? On no, that face, I'd die if I saw the devil's face, let's ride like hell matey let's shake the bastard off! Too terrified to turn round he looks at the reflection for a third time – and laughs with relief. It's only you, you daft bugger, reflected twice in the shop's doors! Talk about paranoid.

The lights are green now and he rides off. Glad I don't have to go at 90 miles an hour, glad I don't have Old Nick's claws clinging to me. Satanic laughter as I pump at the handlebars. Go, you bastard, go! I'll choose my own way . . .

# *A purge on paranoia*

There's a shop by the Post Office which used to sell army surplus stuff when Sue first moved to North London. It didn't last long. It was replaced by a boot-and-shoe repair business – that lasted about a month. Then an antique dealer tried his luck, but he couldn't drum up any custom either and one day he left as quietly as he'd come.

Sue reckons she'd rather move into a haunted house than set up a business here. But there seems to be no end of people willing to blow all their savings on some futile enterprise. Just last week the shop re-opened, this time selling second-hand books. It's always been empty when she's passed by before, and she hasn't dared enter for fear of receiving some lengthy sales talk; but today she can see half a dozen other people browsing, so she steps inside.

The central display is a table covered with books about the Royal Family and England's Heritage. She glances at a glossy biography of Prince Charles, then quickly averts her eyes. How embarrassing if I was seen! I'll steer clear of the Photography shelf (arty nudes for the terminally repressed) and the Theology section too.

The Fine Bindings shelf turns out to contain some of the worst bindings in the shop – decaying crumbly dusty leather which disintegrates at a touch. Sue picks out a book called *My Life and Peregrinations* by Thomas Winchelsea, and opens it at random.

Let me repeat my condemnation of the stinging wasps

> of Rome – that contaminated crew of cutthroats and sorcerers, the papists. Their interest is more in gold than in God, and it may be truly said that they have yielded unto the Divel; for whereas Our Lord did resist the Divel; who offered Him land and riches, the hissing papists have entered a confederacy with Satan, and do desire to subdue the entire World and fill it with their knavish blasphemies.

Waste of a good cow.

She moves on, leftwards, and finds a stack of books about medicine and disease. *The Thalidomide Story. Feel Slimmer, Look Better.* She picks up a volume called *Blackhead's Medical Dictionary* and looks up 'paranoia' in the index. It's an old book and it's not mentioned.

Now a glossily bound book about geriatrics catches her eye. Trying to take it from the shelf she fumbles and drops it, narrowly missing the feet of the woman next to her.

'Sorry,' she says, stooping to pick it up.

'Sorry,' says the other woman, doing a little side-step.

The book is subtitled *An Illustrated Guide to Old Age* and Sue opens it with interest. Dope smoking always makes her feel geriatric – clumsy and shivery and uncoordinated and vague. There are some charts on the main causes of death among 70–80 year olds, and a long chapter on senility. Sue often fears that she's becoming senile, although she's only 20 – she suffers from loss of memory, especially when she's been smoking too many drugs, and recently she's been finding it a strain to read serious books, the sort of stuff which would've presented no problem to her at school. She wonders what's the lowest recorded age for someone to go senile.

She's lost in thought when suddenly a head bobs up in front of her. 'Hey Sue! I didn't realise it was you! Fancy meeting you in here.'

With a look of concentration Sue focuses her eyes, then exclaims: 'Di! Where did you spring from?'

'I've been standing here next to you – but I only just recognised you. It's been so long!'

'Yeah! What're you up to? Still living with that bloke, Colin?'

'Yeah . . . Oh, I found a job! Did you know? I'm working.'

'Yeah? Incredible! What're you doing?'

'Well, I'm selling life insurance, in fact . . .' A young man behind them emits a violent 'SSSH!' so Di carries on in a whisper – 'Look, we'd better not talk in here, why don't you come back for a cuppa tea? Hey . . . What's that book you were looking at so intently? I'll buy it for you.'

'Oh, no – '

'No, let me buy it for you. Don't turn down the offer, you never know when I'm going to be feeling so rich again!'

Sue forces a laugh. 'Oh well, if you insist . . .'

The book turns out to cost £5.50, which makes her feel even more uncomfortable. She gets the bookseller to wrap it up, and then tucks it under her arm and hopes that Di won't mention it again as they walk back to her flat.

Oh well – maybe she'll think I'm doing research . . . or voluntary work in the community with the elderly . . . but probably not. Probably she knows I'm just stoned.

Colin stubs out a cigarette and lights another. For the last ten minutes he's been shaking his head so much that he's becoming dizzy, so now he leans back in his chair and starts tapping his feet instead. 'Tut tut.'

When Di and Sue come in he barely moves. 'Bloody BBC make me bloody sick,' he says. 'They just said "Dennis Healey has made a *bitter* attack on the Tories" but five minutes ago it was "Norman Tebbit made a *strong* attack against the Unions". They just twist language, you know, to put their views across.'

'Hi Colin,' says Sue.

'Oh hi Sue,' he replies, and carries on listening to the radio.

Di goes into the kitchen to put on the kettle. 'Sit down Sue,' she says when she returns. 'You haven't been here for ages, have you? Had we painted the walls when you were here last?'

'Yeah. But all this is new, all these newspaper cuttings . . . You hoping to do the whole room like this eventually?'

'Hmm. I don't know about that.'

'She's just jealous,' Colin butts in, 'jealous of my good idea. You like it don't you Sue. See? Sue likes it.'

'I'm trying to brighten it up a bit with those photos and posters . . .'

'But she's messed up the whole design,' Colin interrupts again. 'I had all this carefully worked out, and then she comes and plonks her pictures wherever she wants, just anywhere, without any regard to the basic design. See – there's two distinct sections, that's the bad news over there, the warning side, and the better news is that wall, that's the looking on the bright side. But can Diane grasp that, oh no. So not only does she have to put up a picture of the Pope, she insists on putting it up on the *good* side, right next to that story "Pop Singer Claims to be Antichrist," when everyone knows that if the old fart has to be up there at all, he should be over *there* with all the other villains.'

'It's artistic where it is,' Di says, 'though I know you couldn't be expected to understand that. I'm just trying to make the walls a bit interesting.' Then before he can reply she disappears into the kitchen again.

Colin lights another cigarette and turns up the radio.

*This is said to support President Reagan's belief that the world recession is coming to an end . . .*

'Hahaha! What!' Colin explodes. 'I thought he was going to say, "Ronald Reagan's belief that the world . . . is flat". Honestly. That's the sort of thing Reagan comes out with, isn't it?'

'Yeah, he believes in Adam and Eve too,' says Sue.

'Yep, mind you you wouldn't expect him to believe in evolution, since he's an ape himself . . .'

'Oi. I resent that. I like apes.'

*A man has been gaoled for a week for whispering in the public gallery of number two court at the Old Bailey today.*

Di returns with the teapot and cups, and says: 'Colin, why don't you ever switch that radio off, it really gets on my nerves sometimes.'

'What? Why don't you ever do anything but complain?'

'Because you never do anything but listen to the radio.'

'Well, somebody has to. You should be glad. You've got to keep in touch, I reckon, otherwise you never know what the bastards are up to.'

'At least turn the volume down, can you?'

Colin exhales deeply. 'Oh alright.'

Sue says: 'So tell me about this job you've got. How did you find it? Is it okay?'

'Can't complain I suppose. It was quite funny, I was walking down Oxford Street and this bloke came up to me trying to sell me life insurance, and when I told him I was unemployed he started trying to sell me the job instead. So I decided to take it. The money's not so bad, but it's been so fucking freezing all winter . . .'

'How 'bout you Sue?' Colin breaks in. 'You working yet?'

She shakes her head. 'And you?'

'No, but I'm keeping busy, that's the main thing. Cigarette? So long as you don't become a vegetable, that's the danger. You still living with that bloke with the long hair, what's his name?'

'Ratty? Yeah, he's still at the flat. And Dan.'

'He smokes much too much pot that geezer does. It's not good for you, specially when you're unemployed. I hope he's not a bad influence. How much d'you smoke Sue?'

'Oh not a lot. Sometimes – no, I hardly ever smoke these days. It makes me paranoid for one thing.'

'Yeah, shit, and there's too much of that around, isn't there. Paranoia I mean.'

'Mm, what, twitchy hippies with stories of persecution you mean . . .'

'No, I mean in the world, there's too much paranoia in the

world. Between countries . . . in politics . . . in the media . . . Everywhere. Straight people are the worst. I mean paranoid about Russia, bloody KGB plots, spies, all that bollocks. Or how the Labour Party wants to turn the country into a totalitarian state. So the last thing we need is *more* paranoia!'

'Yeah, you've got a point there. Ha! Looks like Ratface is barking up the wrong tree then.'

'Eh?'

'Oh, nothing, just Ratface was going on about how dope makes you relaxed, and how it's a good cure for all the aggression in the world . . .'

'Agh, typical! I really hate people like that, people who reckon they've found the meaning of life in drugs. They just can't face reality. Look – ' He indicates the cuttings on the walls. 'This is reality.'

'Well, Ratface . . .'

'He's just a brainless cunt, isn't he.'

Sue sips her tea and feels herself getting hot with anger. How dare you use language like that, how dare you insult my friend, you lazy slob. Colin leans back further in his chair and lights another cigarette. At last Sue can't contain herself any longer. 'Well at least he's *doing* something about it, at least he's not an armchair politician.'

'What? What d'you mean, you calling me lazy? What about you then, you're an armchair politician if ever there was one, sitting around and nattering on your women's rights committees.'

'No, I left them, in fact,' Sue says indignantly.

'So what d'you do now, sit around getting stoned and drinking tea, yeah?'

She slams down her cup and glares at him. Christ, you don't know how lucky you are, you don't know how lucky you are that Di's here. Otherwise I'd fucking kick your teeth in. Pig. How can you stand him, Di? He must be good in bed, 'cos sure as hell he's not good for anything else.

Di's drinking her tea; her face doesn't give anything away.

Sue turns back to Colin and says: 'For your information, I don't sit around and get stoned. You'd be surprised at what I do. I left the women's committee because it was all talk – and I agree with Ratty, I think it's time to stop chatting and start *doing*.' She finishes her tea and stands up. 'Thanks for the cuppa, Di. I'd better be off. See you around, huh.'

Di's expression still doesn't change. 'You off then? Nice to see you. Keep in touch won't you.'

Colin waits for the front door to shut before saying, 'What did she mean d'you think, "You'd be surprised at what I do"?'

'I don't know, but she mentioned that before, I remember – saying how these committees do nothing but chat, and how impatient she was getting.'

'So you reckon she's resorted to direct action of some sort? She's certainly crazy enough.'

'Could be.'

'But she's wrong, you know. If she's breaking the law she'd better watch out. You never achieve anything by breaking the law. Here, I was reading this article . . .' Without rising, he pushes back his chair and hunts through the stack of newspapers on the table behind him. 'Yeah, this bloke, Jerry Macklin, former hippy spokesman and acid-head, 'snow working for the US Government. Says he wants to "work to change the system from within". Says "you can't go on for ever banging your head against the wall. In the end you've got to knock on the door and ask them to let you in". See?'

'Mm . . . Yeah . . . Mind you, there's not too many doors being opened at the moment. And there's a hell of a lot of people banging on the walls.'

# *Family favourites*

It's stopped raining by the time Chris reaches King's Cross, but he's soaked to the skin and he's not sorry that he decided to stop work early today. It's Saturday evening, anyway, so all the tourists will be in their hotel rooms preparing to go out.

Perhaps there's a trade to be done outside the theatres in the West End . . . Postcards? Popcorn? Perhaps he should set up his own theatre ticket agency – he could start small, with just a few tickets. But tonight he deserves a rest. It's been a hard day, although he only did one tour, and even then he had to refund half the money because the woman didn't agree with his version of history.

Chris turns into Alameda Square, and a young girl approaches him and says, 'D'you want a bit of company?' No thanks. Oh what? Chris hasn't suspected, oh dear oh dear. How sad, and in this weather too.

The guest-house door is on the latch. Chris goes in – ah, there's no one at the desk! Very unusual. Maybe he'll be able to slip by, maybe she'll forget . . . But Mrs Greenhorn appears up the basement stairs as soon as he shuts the door behind him.

'I have to remind you, Mr Roberts,' she says very precisely. 'We must have payment in advance. I must have your money now if you want to stay another night.'

'Yes, yes, of course.' Silly old bag, Chris thinks, she's already got £10 of my money as a deposit on the key. Doesn't she trust me or something? But he feels in his pocket and gives her a crumpled fiver. He's down to his last £12 now. 'I wasn't trying not to pay, you know.'

'No, no of course not, no chance of that.' She tucks the money away safely in her purse.

'Things aren't going that well, that's all. I hoped I'd be earning a proper wage by now, but it's not easy to find work.'

'I don't suppose it helps being a Welshman,' says the landlady. 'No offence meant, but there's a lot of anti-Welsh feeling these days, what with holiday homes being set on fire and such. Not that I think you're personally responsible, don't get me wrong – and don't think *I'm* prejudiced, because I'm a reasonable woman, but I know of a lot of folks that are.'

'Well that's their problem not mine,' Chris replies. He wonders whether to go up to his room and put on something dry, but all he's got to change into is a pair of overalls, his old work clothes. So he goes into the lounge to see if he can dry off in front of the fire. But the fire is already being hogged by a couple of other guests – a Malaysian-looking guy, and a tall, blond American who's berating him.

'You mean you don't have Mister Pepper, man? You don't have Bano-Ano?'

Chris sits down on the sofa by the wall and begins to rub his knees. The television is showing a family quiz-show, all bells and glitter, as sincere as a row of false teeth. Almost involuntarily his eyes home in on the screen. At least it means he won't have to make polite conversation to the strangers – he's been doing that all day.

The American, however, is obviously bursting to exercise his vocal chords. Having put the Malaysian in his place, he turns his attention to Chris. 'You man – where are you coming from?'

Chris stares at the TV for a few moments longer, wondering if this is an invitation to explain his philosophy of life. But he says, 'I'm from Wales.'

'Wales? Great, man! I love that accent, go on, do it! Say something to me in that accent.'

'Er . . . like what?'

'Whaddaya mean, like what? Anything!'

'Well then, can you move away from the fire a bit please?'

'Great! Kills me!' he exclaims without budging.

'Er, you're from America, aren't you?'

'Boise Idaho. You know, my gramma was Welsh, came from a town where there's a lot of mining or something.'

'Well, there's not so much mining there now. All the pits are being closed down.'

'That a fact? Jeez, I'd like to go to Wales and find that town before it closes down completely. Car . . . Care . . . that familiar? Hey, there's a lot of sheep in Wales, yeah? I've got a fantasy about getting off with a Welsh shepherdess, boy, wouldn't that be something?' He laughs and slaps his knee. 'Did you ever get off with a Welsh shepherdess, eh? I know what you build those haystacks for! Hahahahaha!'

'Hm. Ha.' Chris'd like to say you're more likely to get off with a Welsh sheep, but he doesn't want to give him any ideas. He tries to turn his attention back to the television.

'In fact it looks like London's going to be pretty good too. Somebody told me that London girls are ugly, but not that I've seen! Wowee! Maybe I'll go out tonight and strike lucky . . . There was some young broad came up to me this evening, just outside the hotel, wanted to take me out . . . ' Yeah, yeah. 'Fox, too.'

'Yes, I suppose she does.' Chris feels disgusted, has this sleazebag taken her up to his room already? No, Mrs Greenhorn would never stand for that. And quite right too. His heart suddenly goes out to his landlady, and again he tries to block Boise Idaho from his mind.

'. . . AND tonight's star prize is a holiday for two in sunny Ibiza! Yes, if you answer the question correctly, you could be relaxing on this beautiful beach' (Shot of bronzed bikinied woman sunbathing). 'Ibiza, where the days are long and hot but the cocktails are long and cool! And don't forget about Ibiza's many interesting sights' (Camera zooms in on cleavage of another sunbather).

'Look at that, eh?' says Boise, impressed. 'Where's that, Ibiza?'

'Anyway it's not in Wales,' Chris says. How thankful he is that his mother isn't watching this! *She* turns pale and switches off the radio if someone so much as mentions 'birth control'.

The Malaysian guest says: 'I want to see a cowboy film. Cowboys and Indians, very good.'

'Better than this crap anyway,' says the American, going to find another channel. 'In the States, in game shows like this, the goddammed *loser* gets a holiday in Ibiza. The winner gets a Cadillac, a yacht, a lifetime's supply of burgers . . .'

And in El Salvador they get an Elvis Presley tee-shirt – but Chris doesn't say that. He says, 'Go on, turn it over.'

On another station a young woman is reading the news. 'Not bad, I like the intellectual type, hey?' He looks at Chris, and sighs when he doesn't elicit any response. Chris thinks: he's probably decided I'm gay, but so what? So long as he doesn't turn violent.

The newsreader announces: 'A team of scientists, led by Professor Gordon Malchick at the University of Texas, has come up with a revolutionary cure for hangovers. They've spent the last three years developing a "miracle drug" which will counteract the after-effects of over-drinking.' Makes you proud, does it?

'Looks like there's no Westerns,' says Boise, turning to the other channels and finding a poetry reading on one and a wildlife programme on the other. 'Looks like it's back to Family Favourites.'

'. . . AND for another £100, what was the name of our second-to-last king? Think about that one – the king before our last king.'

God, there's easy pickings to be made here, Chris thinks. Standing in a nice warm studio, notching up money! I could do that, but I don't suppose I look right. You need to look like that goofy bloke there, I'd have to grow a moustache, and buy another suit – my boiler suit's a bit tatty.

It's always the same though, you need capital! How will I ever afford a suit, when Mrs Greenhorn takes my money faster than I can earn it? I'm going to be out on my ear in a couple of days anyway, unless my business picks up dramatically. I'll be sleeping under a hedge in Hyde Park, and there's no way I'll ever appear on Family Favourites if I'm sleeping under a hedge in Hyde Park.

If only my brother would write . . . He must write soon.

Outside the rain starts again, rattling on the window-panes. The American laughs wrily. 'Looks like I won't be going anywhere tonight. That broad'll just have to wait.' Another silence. 'Hey, d'you have Johnny MacIntyre over here? D'you have anything over here? He's got a joke about English weather. He reckons – what is it? "Britain's warm and dry but not at the same time." Looks like it's true eh. Ha ha ha.'

# *Spreading the weed*

Ratface is re-drawing the badger's tail, with lots of help from Sue. After rubbing it out for the fourth time he turns round and asks Dan, 'Hey, have you got any of that redundancy money left?'

'Caahm on! What d'you mean? I've still got a bit at the moment, but I won't have any in a week's time, that's for sure.'

'Well, if you're going to've spent it all by next week anyway, you might as well save a fiver by giving it to me, yeah?'

'Yeah? No! I'm not loaded, you know. I've got to get a new chain for my bike. The insurance is due soon too, and I've got two parking tickets to pay.'

'Sod the parking tickets! I'm a much better cause.'

'And my road tax is due soon.'

'God, bloody tax . . . I don't know . . . You'll be paying that on the dole too, d'you realise? 'Sgood in a way, you can hold your head high and say "I'm a taxpayer, you know . . . Speaking as a taxpayer . . ." '

'Taxing the dole? They tax bloody everything, don't they?'

'Yeah, you know they're re-naming the tax system,' Sue says. 'They're calling it PAYE, PAYS and PAYD – Pay As You Earn, Pay As You Save, Pay As You Spend, Pay As You Die.'

'Yeah . . . And they have the nerve to call it a free country.'

'Ha! You've been waiting – ' But Ratface is interrupted by a series of knocks on the door and someone shouting – 'Hellos! Hellos! Is there anyone at home?'

Sue tuts and smiles and says, 'Sounds like your friend' to Ratface, who gets up and leaves the room calling: 'Hold on there, be patient can't you, I'm coming.' He opens the door and Harry lurches forward and falls headlong into the passage.

'Hellos, hellos,' Harry repeats as he tries to get up but stumbles again. 'I'm not really drunk, I was just leaning on the door.' He holds out his hand and Ratface takes it and leads him to the kitchen – which isn't easy, because Harry seems to want to go everywhere but to the kitchen. He must be seeing doors in the walls because he's walking into them all the time.

'Ah, I must tell you, I'm very tired,' he says, gasping a bit. When he sees the kitchen he breaks free from Ratty's arms and manages to collapse into a chair. 'Ah, that's better,' and he gives a great yawn and simultaneous belch to emphasise it.

Sue and Ratface, who don't drink, are quite nauseated by the warm waft of stale alcohol which Harry is exuding with every breath. With every 'hellos' too, because there's a few more of those when Harry has made himself comfortable – two each for Sue and Dan and another four for Ratface.

'Are you not drinking tonight?' Harry asks them. He looks around and sees that nobody's drinking. 'Me, I'm not drinking tonight either. Well, maybe a little one. Have you had a little one tonight?'

Ratface says: 'We've had a little cup of tea tonight, that's all. And a little number.' He starts to roll another.

'Ah yes, a little number. Me, I'm like you. With me, it's ALL – ' he pauses ' – or nothing.'

'He's so pissed he's even forgotten he's been at the bottle all evening,' Sue says, and they laugh without any embarrassment – Harry too.

Ratface says: 'I just can't take the booze any more. I used to get so drunk all the time it was like a sort of ritual punishment. It's so damaging to the body, fucks up the mind and makes everything really hard to do. That's just my opinion . . .' Dan nods.

'It's been raining outside,' Harry says. 'I came in here to dry out.'

'You're certainly well soaked,' says Sue. 'Come on, how much you had tonight?'

'I don't know . . . I had a drink at lunchtime . . . A couple of cans in the afternoon . . . We had a bottle of whisky, well, not all of it.'

'A bottle of whisky!' Dan exclaims. 'Christ, I had two pints of lager last night and I've been feeling tender all day. What do you feel like the next day, Harry?'

'Thirsty.'

Ratface shakes his head and lights the joint. 'Look, Harry, this is the real stuff. No one appreciates a good smoke more than you, right?'

'Right, right.'

'Now imagine, if you was an advertising executive, working in one of those plush offices in the City . . . or the West End . . . making up advertising slogans for a living. How would you sell dope to the general public?'

Now Harry looks as if he thinks Ratface is drunk. 'I don't have to advertise it – it sells itself!'

'Yeah, I know . . . But not to Joe Public, you know? Not to the man-in-the-suit . . . or the woman-in-the-suit. How d'you get *them* interested?'

'Launch a big TV campaign,' Dan suggests. 'Sunday isn't the same without a Sunday joint.'

'Or "Smoke the lowest-tar cigarettes – Marijuana"!' Sue says. 'Like that silly Admiral Mild Campaign, "Two weeks of smoking our cigarettes and you won't want an ordinary cigarette ever again".'

But Harry isn't happy. 'Why would I want to deal with that kind of person? He'd just get me busted, for sure.'

Soon Harry's eyes drift shut. Dan puts the kettle on to boil and says: 'Smoking when you're drunk, it's fatal. It just used to make me throw up.'

When Harry comes alive again a cup of tea is waiting for him. He's not really a great tea-drinker, he finds it easier to buy cans of beer; but he takes a few sips. 'I came to invite all of you to a party tonight,' he says at last.

'Great,' says Ratface, 'who is it?' Anyone we know?'

'Des and Dave, they told me to invite you.'

'God, Des and Dave, I haven't seen them for ages. Sure I'd like to go. Mm, I'll take along some of my homegrown.'

'Your new crop's coming along alright, I see.'

'Yeah, no problem. How about you – would you like some sprouts?' He reaches for the tobacco tin on the shelf. 'I've still got a whole bunch.'

'Oh thanks, no thanks, I've already potted mine.'

'How about Des and Dave? Maybe they'd like some.'

'No, I asked them. They're paranoid.'

'Yeah? It's a shame to waste them . . .'

They sit and drink their tea. Sue looks out of the window and says, 'I think it's stopped raining.'

'I need to get a bottle from the off-licence,' Harry announces. 'I feel like getting drunk tonight.'

'Eh! But you're already drunk.'

'That's from this afternoon. I feel like getting drunk again tonight.'

'Well, we'd better go soon, hadn't we? It's almost ten, the off-licence shuts at ten.'

Harry belches again. 'Are youse coming too then, Danny-Boy, Dan-Dan the Action Man? And you, Sue – you too, Suzy-Sue?'

Dan shakes his head. 'Think I'll give it a miss, in fact. I'm not feeling in the mood.'

'No, I'm feeling tired too,' Sue says. 'Thanks . . . but I was out last night, and the night before last, and the night before that, and the night before that . . .'

Ratface produces the road map of London. 'Des and Dave still living in that tower-block?'

'No, they moved . . . Uh, I've got it written down somewhere . . . Ah yes!' He rolls up his sleeve to reveal the words 14 Bolton Road.

'Yeah . . . It's a good walk, think you can make it? Hey, we can go by Wrexham Avenue, you know that posh street with the tidy little gardens out front? We could plant some of these sprouts, I mean I'd hate to waste them.'

Harry agrees, so Ratface puts on his jacket and takes a tablespoon from the cutlery-jar.

'Whaddayawant that spoon for?' asks Sue. 'Cocaine?' And Dan breaks into song – 'Co-o-caine! Fuckin' up ma brain!'

'Course not,' Ratface replies. 'I need something to dig with, don't I. The soil will be like mud.'

'Oops, sorry! Well, good luck with your mission.'

Harry makes it out of the house without any problem, but as soon as the cold air hits him he begins staggering and lurching all over the pavement. Every few yards he stops, draws himself up as if he's about to make some momentous announcement, sways a bit, and then carries on. Sometimes he staggers so much that he almost falls into the road and Ratface has to pull him back. There's not much traffic tonight, but every time a car approaches, Harry seems drawn to the road; and Ratface begins to wonder if he's not doing it deliberately.

Harry buys a small bottle of gin at the off-licence. He opens it immediately and has a swig. 'Grrund, a little gin's all I need to make me see straight. Ah yes!' He makes another dive for the road. 'All I need to see straight!'

'Nah, come on! You can have a rest at Wrexham Avenue.' They'll never get there if Harry takes two steps sideways for every one ahead.

Now Ratface begins to fantasise about the impending planting. Wasn't there some folk hero once called Johnny Appleseed, who used to wander around scattering appleseeds everywhere, and so introduced the apple tree to America – or was it Australia? Maybe Rat could become Johnny Dopeseed, scattering handfuls of largesse wherever he goes! He could start a plague of the stuff. It couldn't be illegal if there was enough of it growing wild, it'd be like making it illegal to grow dandelions.

When they reach Wrexham Avenue, Ratface looks for some

likely spots. 'Careful! I don't want to uproot anything. I want to cultivate life, not destroy it.'

'We could have the whole street in flower!' Harry exclaims. 'What a g-lorious sight!'

'Sssh, shut up eh? Now . . . here's a good spot.' He plants a couple of seeds and moves to the next garden. 'I'm sure the owners will like them – they're fast growing, with a beautiful leaf formation, and very useful.'

In the sixth garden, he says: 'According to my book, immediately after sowing we should water with a fine hose.'

'No problem,' says Harry, undoing his flies and relieving himself on the flowerbed. While he's spraying, a man in a suit walks by and looks very perturbed. 'You don't think he noticed do you?' Harry asks when the man is about two yards away.

The party's well under way by the time they reach Des and Dave's flat. One room has been set aside for dancing, the other for drinking and talking and smoking.

'Do you dance, Ratty?'

'Yeah, but not to this electronic crap. I like the Stones, you know, Deep Purple, something you can fling yourself around to.' So they go into the other room and sit down in the corner. They have a few smokes, and Ratface finds himself drifting away into deep and instantly forgotten dreams.

Looking up again, he finds that Harry has been transformed into a fresh-faced, wide-eyed boy of about seventeen. The boy turns round and stares at him and says very politely: 'Er, is that pot you're smoking?'

Ratty looks down and sees that he's still clutching a half-smoked spliff. 'Oh yeah, d'you want it? Go ahead.'

The boy takes it and lights it cautiously. 'Mm.' Puff puff. 'Mmm.' Christ, is he going to smoke all of it? Hope he has a strong head! When he's put it out, he turns to Ratface again and says: 'What does it do to you?'

'Eh? Haven't you ever smoked it before?'

'No, not really . . . What does it do to you? . . . Er – is it something to do with the teeth?'

'Well, yeah, if you want.'

'Or the toes . . . my toes feel funny.'

'If you want! What about your head?'

'I don't know . . . I can't tell.' But five minutes later he gets up and vanishes.

Now Ratface wonders where Harry's got to. He goes to look for him, and at last finds him lying head-first down the stairs. 'Hey, are you alright?! Hey, you've got to get up!'

'No, no, I'm alright! I've got to lie like this.'

'Wouldn't you be more comfy if you lay straight?'

'No, I've got to lie like this! Oh man, oh man, I tell you, the things I saw . . . Oh, where I've been, it was horrible, oh . . .'

'Where've you been, mate? What did you see?'

'I can't tell you. I tell you . . . Creatures. Touch me. You mustn't leave me. Hey, have you got a drink?'

'No. Why?'

'Get me a drink. Please, if you love me, get me a drink.'

'The last thing you need is a drink . . .'

'My last wish . . . Won't you give me my last wish? I've been to hell, if you'd seen the things I've seen, you'd need a drink.'

'Oh shit. Alright. But don't blame me if you die.' He goes to fetch a bottle of wine, but when he returns Harry is nowhere to be seen. Oh no – he hasn't fallen headlong, has he?

'Are you looking for the old bloke who was lying there?' says a woman in an evening gown. 'I think he went into that room.'

'Over there?' He rushes up to the door and knocks on it violently. 'Hey! Let me in! You've got to open up!'

'Oi! What d'you want?' a woman's voice calls back.

'Er – is Harry in there?'

He hears the woman say 'Is your name Harry?' and then: 'No! Piss off, will you, I don't know who Harry is!'

Oh, dithering dooberries, I hope he's okay . . . I should never have left him! I should've taken him for a walk and made him vomit and cleared his head. Oh, can I forgive myself? Harry! Harry! He goes to look for him outside, but still can't find him.

He's so upset that he decides to have another joint to calm

down. Can't-andle-it-Andy appears as he's lighting up.

'Hey! Rattus! What's happening!' Ratface explains about Harry, but Andy shrugs it off. 'Don't worry about him, eh? He goes to hell and back every night. He can look after himself.'

'Yeah, guess so.'

'Look, let's get down to important matters. I've been wanting to talk to you about this business venture I've thought up which could make us both millionaires. You see . . . Every summer has a fad, right, and this summer's fad is going to be – clinging face-masks in fluorescent green plastic! Whaddaya think?'

# Sunday

## Black economy

Sue bumps into Kevin by the soyburger stall. He waves a clipboard at her and says: 'Hey Sue! Would you like to sign a petition to allow Radio Toucan to broadcast and protest about us having our equipment nicked all the time?'

'Oh no, you haven't been raided again have you . . .' Sue signs her name.

'Yeah. For the third bloody time. They took our transmitter again.' He takes back the clipboard. 'Hm, now would you like to make a donation towards a new one?'

'Ooh. Well. I'm sorry, I'm really skint at the moment.'

Kevin nods stoically and says: 'Aren't we all skint. Radio Toucan especially. The Old Bill, they've nicked hundreds of quidsworth of equipment. They think they can gag us – but I tell you, they won't succeed. We're fighting for the freedom of the airwaves, and, I tell you, you can't hold back the forces of freedom . . . Here, have a badge.' He gives her a handwritten sticker with the slogan 'Save Radio Toucan – 48 metres Sundays'. 'All donations gratefully accepted.'

'Yeah, thanks, I mean I'm really skint.' Sue begins to feel like a fool for signing the petition in the first place, she should've known they wanted her money not her name. 'I never bring any money to the market, I just come to look around.' This is true but it doesn't sound convincing, so she adds – 'Anyway, I might as well give my money straight to the police, don't you reckon? I mean, they'll only come and confiscate your equipment again – don't you think?'

'Giving money to the Filth?' Kevin doesn't understand.

'We're fighting the law. We're giving them a fair old headache, I must say . . .'

Well, you'll give everyone a fair old headache if you insist on playing the Salford Pigs at ten o'clock on a Sunday morning. If anyone actually listens to you, that is. 'I admire your persistence,' she says, 'But don't you ever feel – like just giving up?'

This suggestion obviously outrages him, but he tries to keep his cool. 'Oh no.' Firmly. 'Oh no, I don't think so, we couldn't do that.' Stern shaking of head. 'How would that look, to go under without a proper fight? We'll show these bastards, I tell you, we'll show them.'

Sue wonders how much money he's managed to collect today. Probably not much. Enough to buy him a soyburger or a tofu-cake if he's lucky. 'I'd best let you get back to your petition,' she says with a half-smile. 'Mustn't distract you.'

'Right on. Right on.'

'I'll see you around, yeah? Good luck. I hope you're broadcasting again soon.' And she walks off, thrusting her hands into her pockets to prevent her coins from jangling. She makes for a part of the market where he can't see her. Nothing very interesting down this end though – records, old picture frames, badges and dull printed dresses for pregnant hippies. As she stops to look at some earrings, she hears a voice behind her – 'Hey Sue! What are you doing here? Ha!'

'Hey, Patti! What're *you* doing, you mean! I didn't know you were running a stall! How long you been doing this?'

Patti stops laughing and re-composes her face. 'This is only my second week – but it's going really well! Oh, it's nice to see you. D'you think I'm crazy?'

Sue looks at her table, which must be the smallest in the whole market. Displayed on it are about a dozen waste-paper bins, covered with collages made up of photographs and pictures of all shapes and subjects. On one bin, Fidel Castro rubs shoulders with Bob Marley and John McEnroe and a host of other people Sue doesn't recognise. On another, Sid Vicious is wearing Buckingham Palace on his head and clasping Winston Churchill in his hand.

'No, of course you're not crazy. I think it's a good idea. At least these bins are useful, which is more than can be said for most of the crap here.' She picks up one of the bins to examine it more closely. 'D'you do all this yourself?'

'Yeah. I found stacks of Sunday Supplements and stuff on the rubbish heap, so I salvaged them and chopped them up. I got the bins for 50 pence each too . . . And they're selling really well.'

Sue smiles again. 'They're really professional. They're really neat. Who's this bloke?'

'Er – the Duke of Edinburgh I think . . . What I'm hoping to do, you see, is to print up all the best designs, mass-produce them like. I'm doing a course at the Laveley Workshops. They teach you almost anything – printing, video, pottery, design . . .'

'Yeah? Don't think I've ever been there.'

'You should come along! It's really good. I go on Friday nights, learn about printing and graphics. Why don't you come along? And both the instructors are women.'

'Yeah?' Sue looks more interested now. She suddenly has visions of producing posters, pamphlets, subversive newspapers . . .

'It's really cheap for the unemployed. Vulcan reckons that's just a plot to keep us out of trouble . . . But I don't know.'

'Could be a way for us to make trouble more efficiently. When's this class? Friday night? Might be good.'

Now Patti digs her hand into her top pocket and says: 'Oh shit. I'm out of fags. You couldn't go and get me some could you – a packet of Ardeth.'

'A packet of what?!'

'Ardeth. It's a new brand of cigarette, very cheap.'

'Shit, it's a bit blatant isn't it! I can't go into a shop and ask for our death!' Then, afraid she might've offended Patti, she says: 'If you like I'll look after the stall while *you* go to the shop. Is that a good idea?

'Yeah, thanks. I'll get a bite to eat too, I'm starving. 'You're not in a hurry are you?'

'No, I'm alright.'

'Look. These bins are three quid each, right? You can have half of whatever you sell.' They swap places with a bit of difficulty. 'Thanks, I won't be long.' And she dives off into the crowd.

Sue's relieved to be away from the bustle, she feels safe and superior behind the wooden table. She watches the unending stream of trendies shuffling by. 'Recession chic' is in this year, for those who're working. The clothes are shabby but the faces are still pink and well fed. Dustbin anyone?

A Japanese new-waver stops and inspects all the bins carefully before choosing the most colourful and handing over his three quid. Thank you. Wow, I've made £1.50 already! Not bad for ten minutes' work. Now, if I sold two bins, I'd make three quid . . . three bins is nearly a fiver . . . Yes, this is a profitable business! I could really get into this.

None of this money's going to end up in Kevin's pocket either.

None of this money's going to end up in the Government's pockets either. Buggered if I'm going to declare my earnings! I don't care who calls me a parasite or a scrounger. God – the Government and the gutter press would have us believe it's because of people like me that the economy is in such a mess. They must be mad.

I've got no reason to be ashamed or guilty. In fact I feel proud – proud that I'll be able to go home and tell Dan and Ratty 'I got a job today' . . . or 'You know, I found some work today' . . . Found work, got work – and a quid fifty in my pocket! Makes you proud, eh?

# *Making up the numbers*

First Ratface becomes aware of a pressing pain on his ankle. He tries to move, but his feet feel like spiky blocks of wood and his legs feel as if they're swaddled in bandages. Someone must've been sitting on his head all night, tying up his legs and sprinkling him with a warm sponge.

When he eventually manages to lift his head and look out of the window, he sees the sunlight streaming in. Panic flashes through his mind – Hell! It must be late! When did I go to bed . . . Christ, I was so wrecked, I must've slept for ages.

He tries to move his body once again. Oh shit, that's the last time I fall asleep in my Doc Marten's! His whole body is aching and sticky; all he wants to do is undress and make himself comfortable and go to sleep all over again. But it's much too late to do that. He realises he can't even remember going to bed, it must've been so long ago . . . It must be late, late in the afternoon . . . Or maybe it's Monday! Christ, I was so stoned last night, so tired after walking home, I could easily have slept all day.

He steps out of bed. At least he doesn't have to dress, that'll save a bit of time. He braces himself for the inevitable taunts from Dan and Sue – 'Ha ha, here's Rat van Winkle!' But there's no one else in the flat, and the tea in the pot is stone cold. Where is everyone? Probably Sue and Dan went sloganeering again last night, something daft . . . For sure they've landed themselves in trouble.

But there's still no way of telling what time or even what day it is. The clock in the kitchen has stopped and the batteries in the radio are flat. So he smooths down his hair (which has formed a peak in his sleep) and puts on his jacket and goes downstairs. He doesn't feel like asking any of the neighbours, not face to face, not while he's feeling so dishevelled in brain and body. So he goes out onto the street to try and find someone to ask.

The first person he sees is a young woman, an office worker probably, wearing an expensive-looking blue coat.

'Excuse me, have you – '

But the woman throws him a passing glance and walks straight by.

Ratface feels insulted. Bloody hell, what did she think I was going to do, make an obscene suggestion? I've still got an honest face, haven't I, even if my brain's dead at the moment. He smooths down his hair again. An old lady passes by, but – No, I won't ask her, she'll probably freak out and think I'm a mugger. Then a businessman in a suit, but I can't ask him either, I don't want to be patronised, I don't want him to flash his precision quartz watch at me. So he carries on down the street looking for clues.

Next he sees a young woman wearing a mini-skirt and lots of make-up, tottering towards him on a pair of high-heels. Obviously he can't ask her, people would think he was accosting her, she might think he was hassling her. And close behind there's a black man: but I can't ask him either, not after I've let all these other people go by, it'll look as if I'm a trendy liberal trying to fraternise with our coloured brethren. Another bloke passes by, his eyes transfixed on the young girl's legs; no, I'm not speaking to that creep, anyway his mind's elsewhere and he wouldn't even notice me.

The clock in the laundrette never works. Ratface passes a policeman, but it's below his dignity to speak to a pig unless he's totally smashed and carrying at least an ounce of illicit substances. Besides, you can probably get arrested for asking what day it is.

At last, when he's gone several hundred yards, he sees a young man with hennaed hair and long scruffy overcoat.

''Scuse me – have you got the right time?'

'Sorry, haven't got a watch.'

'D'you know what day it is?'

'Sorry mate, no, I don't sign on for another couple of weeks.'

But an old lady right behind puts down her bags and says: 'Do you want to know the time? It's just gone two o'clock.'

'Do you know what day it is?'

'It's Sunday. I know that because my daughter always telephones me on a Sunday.'

Ratface says, 'Does she, that's nice,' then curses himself because she must be sick of people saying 'That's nice dear' to her all the time. 'Thanks, I'm glad it's only Sunday. You know I think I must be losing my mind.'

'Oh no, you'll know when that happens dear.'

Ratface could turn back now, but he doesn't want to frighten the old lady by seeming to follow her, so he decides to walk on. He's beginning to wake up now, and it's a pleasant enough day for a stroll.

A bus pulls up as he reaches the bus-stop, and impulsively he leaps on board. He's gone quite a distance before he realises that he has no money. But he sits tight, and when the conductor appears he plays for time and searches all his pockets twice and even looks in some pockets he hasn't got. He has nothing but a couple of loose joints and a bunch of keys.

'I'm very sorry, ' he says, drawing out his words. 'I can't understand how this happened . . . This is very strange . . . I'm sure I had some money somewhere . . .'

'Get off,' says the conductor.

'It's alright – I'll get off.'

Soon afterwards another bus appears and he gets on. Again it's a couple of minutes before the conductor appears. This time Ratface assumes a Germanic accent and says: 'Please – I go to Earl – Park.'

'What's that – Earl Park? D'you mean Earls Court or Hyde Park?'

'I don't know. Earl Park. Vair you going?'

'We going Hyde Park mate, we not going Earls Court.'

'Ah! I want – go – Earls Court.'

'Well you'll have to catch a 404 then. Four-o-four. We're not going to Earls Court. *Comprende?*'

'Ah! *Comprende*! Vair I get off?'

'You get off here, matey, and you pay 30 pence. *Comprende?*'

'Uh? No comprende! I get off here . . . sorry . . . *Wilkommen*!' He disembarks a little quicker this time.

But the third bus takes him all the way to Hyde Park. Now he just has to hope he doesn't get the same conductors on the way back.

Practically all the political demonstrations in London set off from or end up in Hyde Park. Ratface remembers one rally here a few years ago when all the traffic in the area was brought to a complete stop. That was a proud moment – although he can't remember off-hand what he was protesting about. Demos become a bit monotonous after a while, the same old slogans and red banners, the same old police helicopter drowning out all the speeches.

Today, however, there are no banners, no hordes of policemen. The campaigning season doesn't get under way properly until later in the spring, when it's a little warmer. But as always there are some specimens holding forth at Speakers' Corner, and he goes over to investigate.

Most of the spectators seem to be young foreigners who're drifting passively from milk-crate to milk-crate and smiling whenever a speaker pauses or raises his voice. Most of the speakers have a religious stance. Some are disputing the existence of God, while others are pouring forth warnings to unbelievers. One is advocating celibacy, another patriotism. And here's a forceful-looking bloke, waving his fists in imitation of a demagogue: 'We must fight for the freedom of the individual, against the namby-pamby nanny State! Today the State forces you to wear a safety-belt in your car – tomorrow they may force you to wear a tarboosh in the greengrocer's!

Make you employ no one but one-legged homosexuals!'

Is that all? There's a lot of activity over there – but it turns out to be an American family trying to read a map. Now Ratface begins to feel cheated. This is Speakers' Corner, isn't it, where people of all creeds and political persuasions can come and exercise their right of free speech? So why's there no one here worth cocking an ear to? I suppose I could make a little speech myself . . . But I haven't got a soapbox, and I'd feel silly just breaking out into a monologue in the middle of all these people, without any warning. The tourists aren't here to listen to speeches anyway, they've come to watch a freakshow, to snigger and point and then walk away feeling superior.

Maybe some better speakers will be along later. In the meantime Ratface decides to take a stroll around the park. There should be plenty to see, on a warm Sunday like this . . . There should be rollerskaters and one-man bands and children playing and lovers necking and people singing and planting marijuana bushes. But instead there's just a few flabby joggers and grim-faced couples walking off their afternoon quarrels.

It seems to be a good time for a smoke. Ratface finds a bench where the police aren't so thick on the ground. After the first few tokes, his brain cells stand up and cheer and clamour for more. A pleasant tingling sensation pervades his body, and all his irritation drifts away like an old memory. The passers-by look happier, and even the police don't look so bad when you're stoned.

Why *don't* I go and make a speech? he thinks. I can't do worse than any of the others. I've got lots of things to say, I could win the crowd round – although I couldn't handle it if the hecklers got too personal, commented on my nose or my trousers . . . And wouldn't someone notice how smashed I am, I mean my head's just doubled in size, they'd be bound to notice that.

His daydream is suddenly shattered by a calm, slow voice beside him. 'Did you expect a plain-clothes detective to sit down next to you?'

'Oh God. No.'

'Well then!' The tone is sharper this time. 'Don't be so furtive with that spliff! Give us a toke!'

Ratface is so relieved that he bursts out laughing. 'What, you're not a cop? Thank Christ for that! Go on mate, finish it off if you like'

The newcomer puffs away. 'Yes, this is very nice. It's a good while since I had a smoke, haven't had any since I came to London.'

'God!' Ratface can't imagine it. 'You're from Wales, are you? Have you just arrived?'

'Ten days ago. I came looking for work, 'cos there's fuck-all where I come from, but it seems there's fuck-all down here too.'

'Too right. I'm unemployed too.' They shake hands. 'I'm John.'

'And I'm Chris.'

'What sort of work are you looking for?'

'Ah – travel courier work.'

Ratface is impressed. 'So what brings you to Hyde Park? Seeing the sights?'

'Er, you could say that. Actually I was more – looking for somewhere to sleep.'

What? Is this guy loaded or what? 'You don't mean – down Park Lane?'

'No. I mean shelter. My landlady's kicking me out tomorrow because I'm skint. I'd go back home, but I haven't even got the money for the fare. So until things pick up – I haven't got much choice where to sleep.'

'What? You weren't planning to sleep in the park? In this weather? Anyway, the police would put you inside. You can't sleep here.'

'My Sunday-school teacher used to say "There's no such word as can't".'

Now Ratface turns and studies Chris's face. He's a bit straight-looking maybe, but that's not necessarily such a bad thing. At least he looks honest. 'Hey, Chris – the place I live . . .

Well, it's not very big, and I share it with two other people as it is . . . It's not luxury, you know.'

'No, no.'

'But it's not bad, I mean it's adequate, there's a ceiling and walls and water and a floor.'

'Yes, yes.'

'I'm just saying.'

'Just saying what? What?'

'What? Oh, I mean if you wanted to stay with us for a while – I'm sure it'd be okay. You could sleep in the corridor, or under the kitchen table – I mean if you're not fussy about crumbs in your bed.'

'No, I don't mind about that! I'm not fussy! Oh, that'd be great. I wouldn't be in your way at all, you know, I'm always out all day looking for work. And if I find work, I'll pay you back for everything. I'll pay you back anyway.'

'Phoo . . . no, don't worry about that . . . I mean, if none of the others mind.'

'It won't be for long, either,' Chris says earnestly. 'Just until I have a bit of money again.'

'Don't worry about it. Shall we go there now, I can introduce you to Sue and Dan.'

'I'd be so grateful . . . I couldn't describe. You've answered my prayers. If there's anything I can do in return . . .'

'Well – yes there is, as it happens. Can I bum 50 pence off you for my bus fare? And if the conductor's a Cockney with red curly hair, I'm a German, right?'

# *Helmet law sucks*

Approaching Buckingham Palace, Dan's mind starts working on how to make lots of money quickly. He could always go to the States and start a new religion. What he really needs is a simple idea which could make him millions . . . Barbed-wire, for instance, that's a useful invention – where would the Queen be without barbed-wire? Or cats-eyes, they're bloody wonderful too, send the bike everywhere when it's wet.

A couple of Rolls Royces pass by. I wonder what the owners did to deserve those? Sod all probably, or they're cigarette barons or directors of drug companies. They can stuff their Rollses anyway, their clumsy fortresses of prestige. Who needs a Rolls? See how obsessively their owners steer them through the narrow streets. No Rolls is ever going to run you down or carve you up, the paintwork is too valuable: the driver sits in trepidation, fearing and avoiding everything around him. You can play a lot of good games with Rolls owners . . .

Not while there are policemen around, though; and today the area is swarming with them. As he enters Trafalgar Square he discovers why. The square is packed full of bikers, and none of them is wearing a helmet. Fair enough, thinks Dan; and remembering Friday night he stops and removes his helmet too.

Some of the bikers are taking part in a triumphant procession around Nelson's Column, shouting and waving their fists, eyeing up each others' machines and girlfriends. Hundreds of other leather-clad individuals are posing by their machines, looking like they're waiting to be photographed. 'Am I dirty enough? Am I dark enough?' Many are knocking back cans of beer, playing at being Hell's Angels – though it's easy enough to see they're not real outlaws. I bet they work 40 hours a week in an office just to pay their insurance. Fag-Ash Joe wouldn't approve of this, oh no. Fag-Ash Joe reckons the flashier your bike, the less of a true biker you are. He reckons the less brain you have, the less you need a helmet. But then Joe and Lil are old already – and most of the people here are afraid of getting old, that's the whole point isn't it? Like that bloke in the pub the other week – 'That's how I'd like to go, no messing, straight under a fucking great lorry.' Buy a car and kill someone; buy a bike and kill yourself.

Most of the slogans are pretty predictable – 'Black Sabbath'. 'Sworn to fun loyal to none'. 'Sucks – Helmet Laws'. A few ugly specimens are displaying swastikas and making fascist salutes. On the south side of the square a car is trying to push past the seething mass of machines, and is being met with blows and insults. A couple of paunchy bikers in Union Jack tee-shirts are sending torrents of gob though the car's half-open window. You couldn't do *that* wearing a full-face helmet.

Still – it takes all sorts . . . Stand up for personal freedom . . . What crap, unless the only freedom you can imagine is death. There's no feeling in the world quite like having your hair buffeted by the wind, and no feeling quite like having your skull buffeted by the tarmac.

Dan puts on his helmet and pisses off.

# *Behind the cover*

Colin's still strange, Sue muses as she pours herself another cup of tea. I hope I wasn't being too unfriendly to him – but then *he* wasn't exactly being very friendly to me, just sitting there and reading the paper and hardly saying a word. At least I was trying to make conversation . . . In fact, I don't know how he had the nerve to come round here at all, after what he said about Ratty and me, about how crazy we were. He didn't even bother to apologise, not in so many words. All he said was, 'I'm sorry we fell out yesterday, here's a little peace-offering.'

It's a funny sort of peace-offering too. Sue unwraps the brown-paper parcel and thinks, I wish Di hadn't wasted her money buying this. What use is it to me? I don't want to depress myself reading about geriatrics. All I wanted was a wee glimpse, and now I've got lumbered with the bloody thing!

She flicks through the book. There's a lot of medical jargon crammed into the large, densely-printed pages. She's glad that she can't understand most of it because it all sounds totally horrific.

I wonder if Colin knew what was in the parcel . . . I'm sure he looked at me funny as he gave it to me. No wonder he thinks I'm nuts.

At the back of the book she finds about 20 pages of black-and-white photographs. She examines them with growing discomfort. She's never seen the naked body of an old person before, never been able to imagine it. She'd always assumed that your skin just became more wrinkled as you got older; she's certainly never dreamed of the extent of the deformities which old-age brings. Breasts which sag down to the hips, stomachs which sag down to the thighs, thighs which sag down to the knees. So that's why old people always swaddle themselves in those shapeless long coats, even in summer – they're not cold, they're ashamed! God, how must geriatrics feel when they see young people flaunting their bodies? Journalists and ad-men saying: 'This is a liberated society, man, let it all hang out!' If a bunch of octogenarians decided to let it all hang out, all those bloody *Tit-Tat* readers would cry into their sparkling white wine.

The sound of voices in the corridor prompts her to cover up the book hurriedly with the Sunday Supplement which Colin left behind. She looks up as Ratface comes in.

'Ah, hi Sue, I'd like you to meet Chris. Chris, this is Sue.' They exchange hellos. Ratty goes on: 'I hope you don't mind if Chris stays here for a few days. He's a bit desperate – he was planning to kip in Hyde Park, so I told him he could sleep in here or in the corridor.'

'Anywhere,' Chris butts in. 'I don't mind. I wouldn't be in the way, and it'd only be for a few days.'

'Hmm. . . How long's a few days? I've heard that before.'

'Look, I'm just waiting for a letter from my brother in the Midlands. I told him I need help, he knows the score. He won't let me down.'

'Okay, okay.' Sue doesn't want to appear inhospitable. 'Course you can stay, for a few days.'

'Oh, thank you! I promise I'll be no trouble. I'll only be here at night, I'm out looking for work all day . . .'

'Huh! Good luck to you. Tell us if you find any.'

'And if there's anything I can do to help . . . I'll clean the house, clean the windows, go shopping. I'm not a dosser, I'll do whatever you want!' He notices the crop of seedlings on the window-ledge. 'I can water your plants . . .'

'Ooh no, not those plants,' Ratface says. 'They're my special plants. There's a special science to watering those, you've got to get it exactly right otherwise it all goes wrong. Leave it to me.'

'As you like. Can't say I've ever tried to grow a crop myself, my mother wouldn't like it. And there's too many English hippies who come to Wales to grow the stuff, so the police have got their eyes open.'

'I'm sorry about that,' says Sue. 'The English hippies, I mean. Must be as bad as India. "Say hello to the new imperialism, same as the old imperialism".'

'Yeah, it's a bit of an imposition I guess.' Ratface shakes his head. 'It's the least we can do in return – invite you to stay here for a while and smoke some of the grass you weren't able to grow. Oh, which reminds me – shall I roll another one? Sorry I didn't offer before.'

'Oh, no thanks, the last one hasn't worn off yet!'

They laugh, and there's a comfortable silence. Sue carries on pretending to read the colour magazine. When Ratface stands up to make a pot of tea, Chris produces a packet of biscuits which was to have been his supper and says: 'Biscuit anyone?' Everyone takes a couple.

Sue's on her third when she becomes suspicious. 'What's in these things? Let's have a look at the packet.' Chris passes it to her, and she reads – 'Flour, sugar, raisins . . . Ugh, animal fat! Pig fat probably! And what's this – ammonium bicarbonate, that's what you clean toilets with isn't it? And what's Emulsifier E322 and Antioxidant E320?'

'Sorry,' says Chris, 'I only looked at the price.'

'Well, I can't eat anything with animal fat in. I'm a vegetarian.'

'So'm I,' Ratface puts in.

Chris doesn't mind. He's munching away steadily – he'll finish the whole packet on his own if need be.

'Well, you won't be eating junk for as long as you're living with us — and no animal flesh!' Sue says. 'I don't allow anything unhealthy in the house.'

Chris hums and haas. 'But I've heard scientists say that some junk food is good for you. So how d'you know what's healthy and what's unhealthy?'

'It's all unhealthy! It's all crap. God, scientists – they'll say anything if you pay them enough. But they all get their comeuppance in the end. There was some geezer in the States known as the Junk Food Professor 'cos he used to appear on TV telling everyone to eat more hamburgers and rubbish 'cos it's good for you.'

'Yes, I think I heard of him,'

'He was murdered a few months ago. Some political activists broke into his house and killed him. Fair enough, I say. If he chooses to sell death and disease and malnutrition . . . I've got no pity for him.'

Ratface laughs and says: 'So don't let's hear you tell us hamburgers are good for you – we stop at nothing!'

'Honestly though, don't you agree?' asks Sue. 'Telling such lies . . . But it's a way of shortening the dole queues, isn't it. It's a way of killing off all the unwanted people in the world. They put cancerous chemicals in our food . . . They contaminate the planet with radioactive waste . . . That's because there's a population problem, they have to get rid of us somehow. And if they don't succeed in killing off enough of us by peaceful means, they'll declare a war and just blow away a whole chunk of the world with a couple of bombs.'

'Well at least you're safe living in London,' says Chris. 'They'll never drop a bomb on London – not with the Queen and all the politicians here. They'll drop it on Wales or somewhere, Glasgow or some other place which they've already bled dry.'

Sue shrugs. 'Well, in the meantime, we just all better mind what we eat. I'm not eating any poison, and I'm not watching anyone else eat it either.' Chris dunks the last biscuit in his tea, and Sue laughs. 'You still want to stay here then?'

'Yeah, of course.'

'Just warning you.'

'You've really saved my life. My landlady's kicking me out, you see – the old bag. Actually I should go back there tonight to pick up my stuff, leave a forwarding address and such . . .'

Ratface reaches out for the Sunday Supplement which is lying open on the table; but Sue pulls it away from him, careful to keep the book hidden. 'Oi! I'm still reading!'

'Sorry! It looked like you'd finished.'

'No. I'm in the middle of this feature about the decline of the British aristocracy.' And she starts reading with a vengeance.

Ratface finishes his tea and announces: 'I smell a bit. I think it's time I had a bath.'

Chris goes off to fetch his stuff.

There's hardly anyone at the station so late on a Sunday evening. Sue walks along the platform, examining the garish advertisements for fashion magazines and holidays in the sun. Funny how the models are still flashing those hollow smiles long after the commuters have all gone home. The women full of naive excitement, and the men so self-assured and debonair. Where do they find all these models, I wonder? I certainly don't know any men who look like that, thank God. Ratty's all scrawny and scruffy, and Dan's only a lad, and now this Chris bloke is a bit of a wimp, too – lucky for him, I wouldn't allow him to stay in the flat if he wasn't, I don't want to be raped or beaten up by some tough desperado.

She stops to read a poster advertising the Jupiter Health Club. 'Men! Get fit and build up your body. Women! Stay slim, stay beautiful.' Sue's appalled. There's no one in sight apart from an old woman at the other end of the platform, and she looks harmless; so Sue whips out a black marker-pen and writes: 'Women! It's time to fight back! Stuff your looks and build up your muscles instead.'

Now she can hear the sound of a train coming chundering through the tunnel in the distance, and a song starts to play in her head:

> We've had enough of male aggression
> It's time to teach the apes a lesson.

The train arrives and the old lady gathers up her bags and

steps on board. Now Sue's alone, and she can set about her task. But surveying the posters the length of the platform, it's difficult to know where to start – they're all so offensive. They're all peddling fantasies to the closeted nine-to-fiver – pictures of tanned women in bikinis to smile at you as you shuffle papers across the desk.

Sue homes in on a poster showing a busty blonde wearing a London Transport tee-shirt with the slogan: 'We're way out in front'. She produces a can of Stic-tite paste from her bag, and a brush, and a black-and-white photograph of a pair of withered shapeless breasts. She's written on it: 'Anyone can sell a young pair of tits, try selling an old pair'. She slaps some paste on the back and sticks it firmly on top of the picture of the buxom woman.

Good, there's still no one coming. Now what about the rest of these photos?

An advertisement for 'Beautiful Bras' shows a woman undressing provocatively. 'Underneath, they're all beautiful' reads the caption. Sue's prepared for this one. She defaces it with a picture of a pit-ridden decaying old body, on which she's written, 'In the end, we're all like this'.

Another poster shows a greasy cowboy leching over the tight-jeaned backside of a woman. Sue plasters another photograph on it – 'Give us back our bodies ♀'. The song continues to play in her head:

All you think about is sex
You use us like a soggy Kleenex.

Du-dum, du-dum, du-dum, 'Just a man, just a man.' This photo! 'This is what a woman really looks like,' she superimposes on a poster of a sunbather lounging seductively in the sand.

She's about to put up the fifth picture when a voice behind her makes her jump. 'That's obscene.'

She spins round and is relieved to find that the man who's speaking is smaller than her, balding and skinny. 'What's obscene? That picture over there of a woman tied to a tree?'

'No, that's nice to look at. Obscene means shouldn't-be-seen. Your pictures shouldn't be seen, they're ugly.'

Sue feels like replying: What about you then, you're pretty ugly too, are you obscene? But she says: 'I don't know, a geriatric man might think it's a turn-on.'

The man persists: 'What if a child sees this? It's disgusting, it's perverted, and it's vandalism. I'll call the guard, I'll call the station manager, I'll have you arrested for vandalising London Transport property.'

Well maybe you should look at this page instead . . . where's that set of diseased ancient pricks I cut out – 'The Officers' Mess'. But at this moment a train roars out of the tunnel and the man looks embarrassed and says: 'Well, I have to go now . . . But you won't get away with this! I'll tell the guard at the other end! They'll be onto you like a shot! Young vandal!' The doors shut on him and he's whisked away into the darkness.

Sue doesn't waste any more time. Her heart is racing as she whips up her last three posters, checking that no one is coming. It's lucky that creepface back there was such a weed; he could easily have been a beefy young drunk itching for a fight. Sue doesn't like the underground at any time, she always finds it stuffy and claustrophobic; but it's worst at this time of night, when seedy, dark-eyed misfits lurk in the smoking-carriages and any man could be a rapist.

Now it's definitely time to get out of here . . . Sue surveys her handiwork for the last time. Yes, this should be enough to wake up some of those dozy-headed commuters on their way to work tomorrow. This should give their fantasies a jolt. Ah, if *I* was awake tomorrow morning, she thinks, I'd like to come here just to look at their shocked reactions: when they see what really awaits them at the end of their working day.

# *Monday*

## *High Street*

Chris groans and turns over as Dan enters the kitchen. 'Ooh, what's the time, the sun's so bright!'

Dan turns on the radio. 'Oh shit, Morning Service.' He flicks it off quickly and says, 'It's only 10.30.'

'Oh heavens! So late.' He sits up, produces a street map from under his blankets and starts riffling through it frantically.

For a moment Dan feels like laughing, but he holds himself back. Keep your distance, boy. He butters a piece of bread and chews it in silence. If you think I'm making you your morning cuppa tea and toast then tough shit. I mean, don't think I'm unfriendly or anything, but I'm fed up with being housemaid to every scrounger who cares to drop by and loaf around for a month or two. Ratface's friends, Christ, Fat Kenny cutting his toenails with the breadknife, and that drunken slob Howard – mind you, *he* was my friend. Was.

'Maybe I should try the City,' Chris says without looking up from his map. 'Are there any tourists in the City? St Paul's, I've read about all those low taverns, yes I fancy that!'

What's he rattling on about? 'Yeah, there's lots of interesting stuff in the City. That where you're going?'

'Ah yes, look at these names, Garlick Hill – the place is reeking of history.'

Dan glances at Chris again, careful not to catch his eye. Must be a student, I'd recognise that jacket anywhere. He switches on the radio again and is fiddling with the dial when Ratface appears in his shirt and pants.

'God, you're late Chris! I thought you said you got up at seven every morning.'

'Yes, I overslept, I'm sorry – I should've been up and out there three hours ago, bringing in the pennies . . .' He stands up and tries to smooth out the creases in his trousers. 'I can't afford to laze about like this . . .'

Ratface makes a dismissive gesture with his hand. 'Ah, don't worry about it! You need a rest I bet. Why don't you have a day off today, put your feet up?' He turns to Dan for the first time. 'You making my breakfast?'

'We haven't got any food.'

'What! You're joking. I got some bread on Saturday.'

'Big deal. I just finished it.'

'Well it's not my turn to go shopping. I bet it's not Sue's turn either.'

'Yeah yeah yeah, I know. I'll go.' He stands up, glad for a chance to leave the house. 'You got some money for me then?'

'Oh, no, my dole doesn't arrive till Wednesday . . .'

'Oh well. I'll have to raid the rent tin again. It's – '

'I'll come with you!' Chris bursts in. 'Let me come. You can show me where everything is, see, then I can do it on my own next time.' And Dan starts thinking – What next time? How long are you planning to stay exactly? The mattress under the table isn't going to become a permanent fixture, I hope.

But he cheers up the moment they step outside. Chris shows himself eager to please and strike up conversation, and Dan warms to him. This Welshman really isn't such a wimp after all, despite his appearance. He has a reckless streak in him, and a warped sense of humour behind that innocent facade.

Chris's jaw drops as they enter the supermarket. 'This place is huge! How d'you know where to find anything?'

'You don't. The idea is that you go around the whole shop thinking ooh, I'll have this, and this, and this, and you end up getting all this crap you never wanted. And then when you come to pay for it all you find a pile of slimming magazines on sale, but it's too late by then.'

'Well, I've been warned about what we're allowed to buy,' says Chris, looking at the well-stocked shelves. 'Baked beans are healthy aren't they? What about this bread?'

'Oh no, don't touch any of that ! Those fruit drinks are full of crap too, carcinogenic . . .'

'Why d'you bother to come here at all then, if everything's inedible?'

'Well, it's not *all* bad. I mean, it's cheap and handy . . .' A runaway shopping-cart delivers him a sharp blow on the elbow. 'But I gotta admit – I do *hate* this place.' . . . The glaring lights and the frantic tussle of trolleys through the narrow alleyways . . . most of all he hates seeing young mothers beating and shouting at their infants – Hands off! Don't touch! Thwack! Be quiet! Thwack! Dan registers every knock and harsh word with a feeling of silent outrage, a shared sense of helplessness. Well, *he* can't talk. What does he know about bringing up children? He'll definitely never have any children of his own.

They queue up at the checkout behind an old lady whose basket is full of cat-food and whisky. 'It's like lining up at your medical, this,' says Chris. 'Everyone feeling self-conscious about what they've got . . . All that chocolate! All those potatoes! All that bog-paper!'

'Luckily *we've* got nothing to be ashamed of.'

The groceries come to over £12. 'But we haven't finished yet,' says Dan. 'There's a shop down there on the left, where they sell nice vegetables and more healthy stuff. Free-range eggs too.'

The grocer's store is empty apart from a stout middle-aged woman who's berating the young Indian behind the counter. 'My husband was just furious!' she's saying, brandishing a bag of peaches and a tin of asparagus tips. 'Look, these peaches are as hard as rocks!'

The store-minder takes one of them and examines it in silence.

'I tell you, my husband was hardly able to contain himself.' the lady raves. 'He told me to take back everything I'd bought here. Look it's all hard!'

The Indian shakes his head. 'I'm sorry madam, but I think

you'll find that most of our goods are of the highest quality.'

The woman isn't even listening. She takes a tin of pineapple out of her bag. 'Hard, this as well . . .'

Chris and Dan are watching the scene in amazement. 'Of course it's hard, it's a bloody tin she's holding!' Dan says, just loud enough to make her half-turn round in disgust.

'It's just not good enough,' she goes on. 'It's people like you who're destroying the good old English corner-shop – selling bad food at outrageous prices. No wonder people go to supermarkets instead. I normally go there myself, but on Friday I was in such a rush that I came in here, and oh what a mistake! Everything completely inedible! I mean look at it all. What can I possibly do with it?'

Chris can't control his temper any longer. 'You can stick it up your bum if you want,' he blurts.

'Or better still stick it up your husband's bum,' Dan suggests. 'Tell him to be grateful and happy with what he's got.'

The lady flushes red. 'Are you threatening me? You filthy layabouts with your filthy language! I ought to call the police and have you arrested for threatening behaviour.' She turns to the shopkeeper again and snatches her peach. 'And I'll report you to the Office of Fair Trading! You can't tell my husband to eat bad food, you won't get away with it!' And she storms out of the shop.

The man behind the counter looks at Chris and Dan and grins. Chris says: 'I hope we haven't lost you her custom . . .'

'She can stick her custom,' says the Indian.

'It's an old English custom,' Dan explains. 'Being rude to people who can't answer back.'

'I know all about your English customs. I've never seen the woman before. She's probably trying on the same game in Mr Iqbal's shop down the road.'

Dan rushes round the shop, quickly filling his basket with vegetables and other groceries. This time the whole lot comes to only £1.90. He produces a pound note and a jangling pile of silver and copper. 'Sorry, but I have to get rid of some of this, my trousers are falling down.' He counts out the correct amount, mainly in two-pence pieces. 'Funny, you could never find two-pences when you needed them for the phone-box, now the place is awash with them.'

Chris steps out onto the street a little nervously. 'I was afraid she was going to be waiting for us . . . going to pelt us with her hard peaches . . .'

'Phoo!' Dan chuckles. 'God, some people haven't got anything better to do than complain, have they? It was the same when I was working for the ticket agency – people were always so rude if you couldn't give them exactly what they wanted.'

A smell of frying wafts into Chris's nostrils and sends messages to his brain. 'You know, all that healthy food is very nice,' he says, 'but I don't half feel like loading up with a good dose of junk food before we go back. Want to join me?'

'What, go in here you mean? Have a Kingburger?'

'Yeah, why not? See what they've got anyway.'

As they enter, Dan laughs and says: 'I hope Sue and Rat don't see us! They've got a thing about Burger Palace, they really hate it.'

Chris looks at the pictures of hamburgers above the counter. 'Why, what's wrong with it? Looks okay to me.'

'Well, for one thing they reckon the meat's physically addictive, because of all the tranquillisers and steroids and chemicals the animals are pumped full of before being slaughtered. I can believe that, you know, when I see kids yelling and screaming "Mum, mum, I must have a Kingburger, wah! Wah! Gimme a Kingburger!" . . . Plus the meat's all just minced eyes and bollocks anyway.'

Chris winces. 'What! No thanks! They don't say that on the menu. Think I'll just have a bag of chips, then. Want to join me?'

'Yea, alright. I think the chips are made out of real potato.'

But Chris isn't happy when he finds that all his 80 pence buys him is two tiny pouches with a few skinny chips poking out. 'What's this?' he asks Dan as they sit down in the corner. 'A sample?'

'Disgraceful isn't it. That's why I never come to these places – it's just so bloody expensive! I mean, I'm not as ideologically sound as Sue and Rat – I'm a crypto-vegetarian I guess, I mean I like a bacon sarny now and then . . . But this place is a rip-off. No wonder they're so stinking rich. You know they gave millions of dollars to Richard Nixon when he was running for President, they gave millions of dollars to Ronald Reagan too.'

'God! Why didn't you tell me all that before we came in?' He finishes his chips and dismantles the pouch in a vain search for more. 'Now I'm hungrier than when I came in! Those three-and-a-half chips have just got my appetite going.'

'Hey, look at that bloke over there, he looks like he lives on this stuff . . .'

But Chris isn't listening; he seems to be staring at Dan's knees. Dan looks down, and sees a water-pipe which runs into the seat's wooden front through a roughly cut hole.

'Eh, budge up.' Chris stands up and sits down next to Dan, then starts rummaging through the shopping bags under the table. 'Yeah, here they are!' He takes two eggs out of the carton; and checking that no one's watching, he crams them through the hole. There are two muffled splats as they hit the floor beneath the plastic padded seat. 'Ready then?'

Dan emits a cackle. 'You're crazy!' he says as they walk out. 'Why did you do that?'

'Because Burger Palace stinks, and if it doesn't now, it certainly will in a few days!'

# *Making waves*

The house is empty when Ratface returns from the shops, but he can see that Chris and Dan have been back in the meantime because the fridge is full of groceries. But that's strange . . . how come there's only four eggs in the rack? Have they had lunch already, or did they go out to greet our local MP?

He switches on the radio and tries to find some good music. This banal dirge will never do, I want a bit of classical music . . . Something rousing and grand, something to inspire the plants to grow tall and strong. A bit of Wagner would be ideal. Yes, fine. Now what can I do? Make a cup of tea perhaps . . . a little dusting . . . I've already washed my towel and clothes before I set off. What else can I do? I'd better have a smoke and think about it.

He's puffing away pensively when there's a frenzied attack of knocking at the front door. What's this? Someone forgotten their key? No need to panic, I'd've thought. The knocking continues and he shouts: 'Calm down, I'm coming!'

'My flat's flooding!' a woman's voice yells. 'There's water dripping from my ceiling!'

Ratface freezes when he recognises the voice. It's Mrs Marvin from Flat One, she can't come in here! Not with all the plants in the kitchen, that's the first place she'll go if she's looking for a leak. So he calls out: 'Hold on, I'm in the bath!' and rushes back to the kitchen, trying not to make any noise.

What a fuss, eh, it's probably only the cat pissing from her lampshade. He decides to hide the plant tray in his bedroom, but as he kicks open the door he sees a huge puddle in the middle of the floor where his washing has been dripping. Oh shit, what do I do now?! He rushes into Sue's room and hides the plants under her bed. Then he heads back to the door, which is starting to resound again with knocks.

But – oops! I hardly look as if I just stepped out of a bath, do I! So he takes off his boots and socks and pullover and undoes some buttons on his shirt and splashes some water on his hair. That's more realistic. He takes a deep breath and opens up.

'You took your time didn't you!' Mrs Marvin says crossly as she storms in. 'I was about to break the door down, I'm afraid my whole ceiling's going to give way. What have you been up to?'

'I'm sorry,' he says, leading her to his bedroom, 'just my washing.' A whiff of grass catches his nose and he swings his arms vigorously to try to clear the air. 'I'll get some sponges.' When he returns she helps him clear up the mess with a tight-lipped expression. Ratface feels a proper fool – he wishes he'd hidden his soaking clothes as well – and he apologises copiously.

Mrs Marvin doesn't say a word until the floor is dry (and looking cleaner than it's done all year). She says, 'If there's any damage I'll send you the bill.' Then she strides off, and Ratface wonders if there's time to slot in a couple more sorries. As she opens the front door, she glances into the bathroom and sees the bath completely dry. She looks round and says, 'What *were* you doing in the bath exactly, seeing there's no water in it?' and then slams the door behind her.

Now Ratface feels even more ashamed. What'll she think I was doing in the bath without any water? I bet her fevered imagination's running wild . . . she'll think I was practising black magic or some solitary sexual perversion. She'll probably tell everyone – shit, these people are so paranoid they might even tell the police!

Ratface doesn't like any of the neighbours. They're all middle-aged and stuck-up and think you're a lawless layabout just because you sometimes listen to pop music on the radio. In the early days, none of them even responded to his hellos in the hallway. One night he actually confronted Mr Benson on the stairs and said straight out – 'Why don't you want to talk to us, have you got bad breath?' And Mr Benson replied equally brazenly, 'Well we're not used to living in the same house as a bunch of kids on social security.' Mind you no one's ever brought that up again, not since Mr Benson and Mrs Marvin and Miss Puddifoot all lost their jobs within three months of each other.

He hangs up his clothes in the bathroom. So what if Sue doesn't like my pants, I'm not going through all that again. What if that had happened later in the summer, with the plants all five-foot tall in tubs weighing 20 pounds each? How would he have shifted and hidden them all then?

Last year he went through that rigmarole about a dozen times, for the gasman, the electrician, people like that. But it's all a hassle. And it's pathetic really, having to perform that ritual every time, yelling excuses through the door, when if he really had the courage of his convictions he'd come straight out with it and say, 'Yes, I am growing some plants, what's wrong with that?' I mean, it's no good pontificating about the weed if he can't even be honest with the people he shares the house with. He should've given the joint to Mrs Marvin, he should've said, 'Suck on that, how d'you like it, you can have some more when this lot's ready!' Now, that *would*'ve been progress.

Because – what's he really achieving, just smoking with himself and his friends? Who's he kidding? Sometimes, when he's very stoned, he thinks: All this smoke must be going somewhere, it must be building up in the atmosphere, if everyone smokes enough there'll soon be an appreciable marijuana content in the air we breathe. But when he's straight he knows that one juggernaut can belch out more smoke at one set of red lights than a whole crowd of hippies at a rock festival can do in a whole weekend.

Maybe Sue's right – maybe I'm just crazy. Or lazy. Or a hippycrite. Christ, I can't even get it together to finish my drawing on the wall . . . I can't even decide whether to finish it.

On the radio, the opera has given way to a chilly-voiced drama presentation. *'I am not sorry that you missed the flight, minister, for your presence in London enables us to investigate you more closely. Ha ha. There is a dinner party at Lady Flavia's tonight. I hope you will do the gentlemanly thing and come – unarmed.'*

# *Poisonous turkeys*

'A waste of time. A total waste of time.' Sue takes off her coat and shoes and slumps into the chair. 'I don't know why I bothered to get all tarted up like this. The bloke didn't even look at me till I got up and left.'

Outside there's a crack of thunder followed by the sharp rapping of rain on the window-pane. 'Sounds like a funny sort of interview, if the bloke didn't even look at you.'

'Well, for a start there were about twenty other people there, all men. And this fat bloke came in and told us that we could all be millionaires in twenty years time if we set our minds to it – going on about fast cars and company holidays in Las Vegas. He was chain-smoking too, ugh! But he didn't even tell us what the job was until he'd been crapping on for about half an hour. He said, "You'll have to give up your social life, you'll have to dedicate yourself totally to the job if you want to succeed. We make sure we weed out all the slack-arses and part-timers. But if you want everything I've got, then you can do it – selling encyclopaedias." '

'Selling encyclopaedias!' says Ratface. 'What a con!'

'Then he said, "Anyone who wants to leave can leave now. Let's not waste each other's time." That's when I stood up and left. I thought I was going to be the only one at first, but then practically everyone else stood up as well! Everyone but about two people, we all trooped out.'

'Good! What did he say to that?'

'I don't know, but he looked at me with this nasty smirk on his face, like he was really glad to see me go. "Oh no, can't have women, they're too weak and feeble and they go off and have babies." I bet that's what he said, "Now that we've got rid of the dross . . ." But I tell you, if he's the top, then I'm proud to be the dross.'

'Yeah, I couldn't handle a job like that, selling my soul from door to door. I'd feel a right wally! I'd probably get my teeth kicked in, and quite right too.'

'What about me? I'd probably get raped, knocking on strangers' doors . . .'

'Oh well . . . Who wants to earn all that money anyway?'

'Mm, I do! But I don't want to be a blob like that bloke, noshing and boozing and working round the clock – he'll probably die of a heart attack in a couple of years, no next of kin 'cos he never had time to marry or have any friends, and all his money'll revert to the company. What's the use of that?'

'Bugger all.' Ratface's mind is elsewhere now, he's struggling with the crossword in the newspaper. Twenty minutes ago he solved a clue and triumphantly filled it in; but since then he's been completely stuck and his solitary word is beginning to look a bit pathetic. He wishes he'd never started it at all.

'Oh well.' Sigh. 'I might as well go and change. Why don't you put on a cup of tea, I'm parched.'

Ratface is at the sink when Dan and Chris come in, soaked to the skin. They're dripping so much that Rat half expects Mrs Marvin to come rushing up saying that her flat's flooding again.

'We got drenched,' says Dan as he scrubs his hair with the tea-towel. 'Bloody English summer – we get ten minutes of sunshine and then the skies open up and piss down on us like we've just had a three-month heatwave. Bit of an over-reaction.'

They all sit down to recover. After a while Chris speaks. 'You don't have a television, do you? Makes a change.'

'Well, we couldn't afford it, for one. But it's just a bloody great tranquilliser, isn't it. Everyone sitting around watching Big Brother.'

'So what do you do instead – listen to the radio?'

'Mm – maybe. We make our own entertainment, I guess you could say.'

Ratface laughs. 'Yeah! Dan writes – with a spray-can.'

'Oh no, give it a rest, will you? . . .'

But at this moment Sue re-enters and says, 'No, come on, what're you ashamed of? Tell Chris the whole story.'

'Yeah, go on,' Ratface urges, 'I haven't even heard the full story yet.'

So he explains about the *Evening News* and the Ministry of Death and the helmetless ride, but Chris sits so stony-faced during the whole account that Dan becomes embarrassed and concludes by saying, 'Actually it was all such a hassle, and maybe there's not a lot of point anyway . . . Hey Chris, I preferred your idea – '

'*No*,' Chris says emphatically. 'I don't think it's pointless, writing slogans and such, it's one of the few ways we can put our views across to people in authority. I bet the people going into the Ministry this morning . . . I bet your slogan made them sit up and think.'

'Well, probably not in fact . . . The Old Bill had a whole weekend to clean it off.'

'Well, all right, that only means that one slogan's no good, you need a heavy sustained campaign of sloganeering. You need to write essays on the walls, not just words. Books on the bus-shelters! You need to write more than they can ever get rid of! You need – er – '

'You need an army,' says Sue. 'You can't go and write an essay on the House of Commons, it's illegal.'

'Is it? Mmm. In that case – better to be hanged for a sheep than for a lamb, as they say. Might as well go the whole hog.'

'Eh? I'm a vegetarian remember,' Ratface quips.

'Look. Do you know how I've been earning my living in London? I've been giving guided tours, selling postcards and stuff, providing a valuable service to travellers. On Sunday, just before I met you, I was told I was breaking the law. Well, I made up a story of course, and they didn't catch me . . . but if they had, what would they have done to me? I was a criminal. I was selling culture and history, but in the eyes of the law I was a petty criminal. God, not even a master criminal!'

'So what're you saying?' Dan asks. 'We ought to get into serious crime?'

'I'm a vegetarian too remember,' says Sue. 'I'm not in favour of violence . . . Well, only sometimes – to rapists, fr'instance.'

'You needn't resort to violence. There's lots of peaceful ways too.' They all fall silent until Chris says: 'Everyone hungry? I might as well start cooking supper now.'

But Sue doesn't let him change the subject. 'What are these peaceful methods then? Holding a peaceful demonstration? Most of them are a waste of time.'

Ratface says: 'I reckon demos are a police trick – they get people to give up their Saturdays, half their weekends, marching along in full sight of the law like a mobile prison! And everyone acts as meek as mice – when instead they could be out there on their own, *really* stirring things up!'

'Demos are a cliché, that's the trouble. The newspapers don't bother to report them. The public aren't interested unless someone's killed. You need to do something that'll create a stir.'

'Running across a rugby pitch topless,' says Dan. 'That's about the only way to get in the papers these days.'

'The Animal Liberation groups are good in that way,' says Sue. 'They know how to stir up publicity. Like before Christmas, when they announced they'd poisoned a turkey. Stuffed a bird full of poison in a shop somewhere in Britain. Well, it wasn't true as it turned out, but of course it had to be given mass-media coverage.'

'They do a lot of sloganeering too, don't they? The anti-nuclear groups are always so clean, they never dare break the law. But I'm afraid time's running out.'

Chris says: 'You know how some people are waiting for the Second Coming? A lot of other people spend all their time waiting for the Revolution – "Come the Revolution, comrade."

If everyone keeps on waiting for it, it'll never actually happen. Not that I'm advocating revolution – but I think if you believe strongly that something's wrong, you should go out and try to change it.'

'That's exactly how I feel,' says Ratface. 'You can't do much on your own – but you can do your best. You can try.'

'You have to strike where the heart is,' says Chris.

'Hmm . . . That's difficult,' says Sue. 'It's all bound up together – the patriarchal society, male aggression, warmongering and the arms race. Where d'you start?'

'Aggression, due to too much meat and booze and no marijuana!'

'It's big business,' says Dan. 'Greed, powerlust. But it's not only men, the biggest warmonger in the country is Margaret Thatcher.'

'Yes, but she's an honorary man. Probably when she dies they'll discover she was really a man.'

'God. Her and her "Victorian Values". "Cleanliness is next to Godliness".'

Chris says: 'I must say, it's a relief to find some English people who aren't in love with her. I though it was all part of the "English disease", self-abuse.'

'Christ, we all really hate her. Especially when she speaks . . . Every time she opens her mouth, out comes a great pile of vomit.'

'Hmm,' Chris muses. 'That really would wreck her image, wouldn't it.'

'What's that?'

'If she really did puke her guts up in public.'

'Oh yeah! And how would that ever happen? Send her a poisonous turkey for Christmas!'

'No.' Chris leans forward and puts his clenched fists on the table. 'She's got to do it in public. It's got to make a stir, so that she could never be taken seriously again. They say pride comes before a fall . . .'

'So – how d'you make her throw up?'

'Well – my younger brother works in a hospital, he told me about these tablets which induce instant vomiting. If someone could slip her a couple, in her water, at some function . . . making sure there were photographers at the ready.'

'Huh! No one would dare publish the pictures.'

'Whaddaya mean, a great photo like that? It would go down in history!'

'Yeah . . . Now all you need do is get into Mrs Thatcher's personal confidence.'

The others laugh, but Chris looks unabashed. 'You don't have to get into her personal confidence – you just have to get close to her, that's all. It can't be so difficult, at a public meeting. I've seen her on the telly, surrounded by ordinary people – no soldiers or policemen in sight.'

'She uses plain-clothes men doesn't she,' says Sue. 'Probably the whole crowd is bloody plain-clothes men and women.'

'I don't know . . . They always look like senile old fools to me.'

'Well, you don't look like a senile old fool,' says Sue. 'You don't honestly think you could prance into a public meeting and drop some pills in her water without anybody noticing, do you?' Dan and Ratface laugh again, and they all agree – Chris is nuts.

'But until you've got a better idea . . .'

# *Tuesday*

## *Don't tell me about it*

Sue takes up her position outside the Army Careers Office and unfurls her placard. It'd better not rain. After all the work I've put into it, finding a piece of cardboard big enough to hang round my neck, getting the wording and lettering exactly right, the last thing I want right now is a bloody thunderstorm.

It's not that Sue doesn't like mass demonstrations. She's been on quite a few, and always enjoyed watching people's faces and reading their posters and badges and tee-shirts. But always at the end of the rallies there's a sense of anti-climax; everyone drifts off home, the press congratulates the police that there was no violence, and in the end there's nothing but a bit of litter and a few photographs to show that anything happened at all. The speeches have been heard and the slogans read by no one but themselves. So last night she started thinking – how much more impact it would have if people decided to demonstrate on their own, individually and spontaneously; not in one field, for one afternoon, but all over the country, all year round. Not in private, amongst the converted, but in every high street and on every corner, to make people stop and stare, to make them turn around and think.

She looks down at what she's written. The letters are four inches high, some of them are underlined and others are picked out in red.

PUT AWAY THE TOYS, BOYS.
WOMEN – TAKE AWAY THE TOOLS
OF DEATH AND DESTRUCTION.

WE STILL HAVE A CHANCE TO SAVE OUR PLANET.
BUT IF WE WASTE ANY MORE TIME,
WE WILL ALL HAVE TO FACE
THE COMPLETE DESTRUCTION
OF OUR ENVIRONMENT.

At first she feels a bit conspicuous, a bit wary that lots of her old school teachers and acquaintances are going to appear suddenly and make her feel embarrassed. But it's strange how few people are even bothering to look at the sign. Most are just walking straight past without so much as a sideways glance. They don't want to get involved, and they're afraid that just one look might taint them, embroil them in a tangle of commitments from which they can't escape. Who do they think I am, for God's sake! A religious fanatic or a bearer of a huge chain-letter? Perhaps they're afraid that I'll ask them for money or deposit a curse on them and their home. But haven't these people got any curiosity at all? These shoppers and lazy businessmen . . . don't let me criticise, but do they always walk around with their heads stuck up their bums?

A couple of young children appear, play hide-and-seek around her, squeal and grab her legs and then rush off laughing. The young men who pass by, they're more interested in her face than her placard. I really don't like being stared at, but what choice is there? As long as no one turns violent . . . What about that American bloke, that fat little American I saw in Hyde Park last summer who started yelling 'I'm an American GI! I fought in Vietnam, you motherfucker! What you gonna do about it?' and then attacked an Iranian newspaper seller. These army types tend to be irrational.

She watches the men as they pass by. Awkward or arrogant, they all look as if they could turn violent at the slightest provocation. Maybe it's lucky most of them are ignoring her.

But now here comes one whose haughty stride tells everyone of his self-importance. His umbrella clack-clacks along the pavement like a pair of spurs, and he looks at the other pedestrians as if he's inspecting his minions. When he sees Sue, he dons his spectacles and studies her sign as he approaches. Then he grins smugly and stops in front of her. He pauses for a few seconds before announcing: 'You know, all you gels keep on crying about equal rights, but there'll be no equality until you prove you're worth as much as a man. When women fight side by side with men, and when you can fly bombers and fire torpedoes, then there may be equality.'

Sue is filled with contempt. 'We don't want equality to kill. We don't want to fight your stupid men's battles. Women give life, we don't take it away.'

'You seem to forget,' the man says, 'if our Army didn't fight wars, we'd all be in slavery by now.'

'No, *you* seem to forget. If *no* men fought wars, we'd all be living in peace by now.'

The man doesn't have an answer to this, but he smiles superciliously and carries on his way. Pompous git. Thinks his red carnation puts him at the pinnacle of civilisation. Thinks 'There'll always be an England' even when the whole world has been reduced to a smouldering uninhabitable wasteland.

The roads are getting busier now, it must be the lunchtime rush. Some of the car drivers are looking at her placard as they wait at the lights, some of them are grinning at her, she's not sure why. But most of them don't notice her, so she's able to stare at them as they pass by. One in a box, one in a box, surrounded by lots of wrapping, and the bulkier and more expensive the wrapping, the mouldier the contents.

When Sue looks back at the pavement she sees a woman in a fur-coat bearing down on her, walking as fast as her stiff actions will allow. She's only about 40, but her face is twisted with conceit and disgust for her fellow-creatures. She stops and reads Sue's sign, squinting through her narrow eyes. When she starts to speak, Sue's fascinated by the strange contortions she's making with her mouth.

'Oh! I don't know how you have the nerve to display such rubbish, and outside the Army Careers Office as well! You know my neighbour's nephew fought in the Falklands, for people like you to be free to make a protest. He shouldn't've bothered.'

'No, he shouldn't' says Sue.

'You should be glad you have free speech. If you lived in Russia, they wouldn't allow you to do this. Would you like to live in Russia?'

'Would you like to live on the thirtieth floor of a tower-block with mould on the walls and people pissing through the letter-box?'

'Such language! You're unemployed, I suppose. Yes. Well it's disgusting, you should be looking for work instead of lounging around at the taxpayers' expense.'

Lounging around! Sue's already scanned two newspapers today in her search for jobs. Aren't the unemployed allowed any rest?

'Your sign is very provocative,' the woman concludes. 'You ought to watch out, I wouldn't blame anyone who came along and hit you, you little layabout.'

Sue wants to knock her down for this, but instead she grabs her fur-coat and says, 'Well, your coat is very provocative, too. *You* ought to watch out. The last owner was murdered in it.'

The woman gasps and says, 'What nonsense, my husband bought it new!' And she storms off, happy to have had the last word.

The wind turns cold now and Sue's stomach starts to groan with hunger. She's only got a few bob on her. She could go and buy some biscuits maybe, or a packet of peanuts . . . but she'd feel silly walking into the shop with the placard, and even sillier munching away in the street with this thing hanging around her neck.

She wonders: How much longer am I going to have to stand here? I suppose it was a bit optimistic to hope I'd get any reaction apart from insults . . . But it's a start, isn't it? Maybe one or two people will go away and think about it – trainee murderers at the end of the dole queue, the dizzy businessmen in their conference rooms . . . Maybe the snotty woman will even understand what I was saying about her fur-coat one day.

When a policeman appears at the end of the street, Sue knows what's going to happen next. She wonders whether to run off and hide until he's past, but in the end she decides to stand firm. The policeman walks ponderously towards her, stops to read the placard (which takes at least a minute), and then says: 'I'll have to move you on, I'm afraid, or I could do you for obstructing the footway and causing a breach of the peace.'

'Whaat!' Are you crazy? 'I'm not causing a breach of the peace.'

'Not at this particular moment you aren't. But what if a big tough sergeant-major came along and read this and lost his temper? What if he hit you? There'd be a breach of the peace then.'

'Eh? You must be joking! You'd do the sergeant-major then, wouldn't you?'

'Not if you're breaking the law by obstructing the footway. You are a potential nuisance and I must ask you to move on.'

Sue raises her eyebrows in mock amazement, but can't think of anything to say. Alright, alright, you don't have to stand and stare! But he obviously isn't going to budge until he's sent her on her way. So she takes off the placard and rolls it up, very carefully, and then walks away without so much as a word or a backward glance. She doesn't want to give him the opportunity to smile and utter some patronising banality like 'Sorry, love, but I'm only doing my duty.'

# *Oily ones*

Tonio is sitting with Sue and Chris when the others come in. He looks up and says: 'Hey, have either of you got an aspirin?'

'Sorry, never touch aspirin,' says Ratface. 'I don't do anything legal.'

'Fuckin' L, my head really hurts, you know . . . I think I've been working too hard lately.' Tonio rocks back and forth in his chair, rubs his forehead and his stomach. 'God I feel shitty. Guess I'll have to have a cigarette instead.'

'Oi, put those away!' Ratface orders. 'You don't need them, I'm about to roll a spliff.' But Tonio lights one all the same. 'You nicotine-crazed cigarette addict . . .'

He's no longer interested in Rat or Dan; instead he's talking only to Sue, and punctuating his speech with a strange assortment of sighs and groans. 'Have you seen the new James Bond film? Gnnn . . . It's got a really good car chase at the end . . .'

'James Bond?' Sue's tone is contemptuous. 'The last James Bond film I saw was when I was seven.'

'It's really funny, so slick . . . I wouldn't mind seeing it again. D'you feel like seeing it with me some time?'

'I never go to the movies. There's never anything worth seeing, it's just a waste of good dole money.'

'I'd pay, of course!'

'I told you, I never go to the cinema. Sexist crap, most of it is.'

'God! Never go to the cinema, don't have a television, and you're all unemployed too . . . Don't you get bored to death?'

'They make their own entertainment,' Chris explains.

'Whaddaya mean? Have mass orgies all the time, do you?'

Tonio's a bit hopeful here. Sue doesn't react at all, but Chris exhales loudly and says: 'Hey Dan, Sue tells me you're quite a wizard with the scissors. I was wondering if you could cut my hair for me.'

'Yeah, course, any time you want.'

'Like – hows about now?'

'Sure!' Dan laughs. 'What, right here d'you think?'

'Well . . . Maybe in the corridor, in fact, or in your bedroom. It's a bit of a squeeze in here.'

'Alright. It's a bad habit, in fact, cutting hair in the kitchen – we always have hairy meals for a week afterwards.'

So they go into the bedroom, and as Chris shuts the door behind him he says: 'Phoo! That Tony bloke doesn't half go on. He's been yabbering on ever since I got back – about his headache mainly. Saying he's been working too hard.'

'Working too hard my arse! He's been drinking too much, that's all. He's always on the piss . . . I hope you don't mind this sheet, it's a bit oily that's all, I use it to clean the bike sometimes.'

'That's okay . . . Anyway, Tony's not making himself very popular. He's been trying to chat up Sue all evening, it's really embarrassing.'

'Oh well, she's used to it. She can look after herself.'

'Mmm. You know he's asked her out five times already since I came back, and she's turned him down every time!

Dan's already taken a few hacks at Chris's hair before he asks, 'How d'you want it?'

'I was hoping for a good respectable sort of haircut. Something very traditional if possible.'

'If that's what you want. Sure you don't want something a bit trendy instead, how about a nuclear warhead?'

'I'll tell you why. You see, I've found a Conservative Party meeting tonight in Piccadilly . . . somewhere . . . and I want to go along. Get the lay of the land sort of thing.'

Dan cackles loudly. 'Well, if you want to look like a Tory,

you'll need a very special haircut. It needs to be long at the front, short back and sides, and lots of long strands across the top. D'you want a bald patch too?' Clip, clip.

'I must say I've always been a bit innocent about politics,' Chris says. 'I've never really kept abreast with what's going on at Westminster, it doesn't mean a lot to us in Wales. And the political parties – I mean we're meant to have a choice, but I can't see much difference between them myself, they all seem to be a bunch of old stooges.'

'Yeah, it's true, they're all just doddering old men. Even the Opposition never actually *does* anything. God, if I was in Parliament, I'd always be kicking up a fuss! I'd really like to get things moving, I'd create fucking hell!'

'Well why don't you go into Parliament if that's how you feel?'

Dan blushes. 'Oh, come on . . . Who'd vote for me?'

'Well, I would! If I was able to vote, that is.'

'Can you imagine me campaigning? Most people cross the road to avoid me as it is! They'd never open their doors to me; call the police more like! These are the only clothes I've got, my jeans and bike jacket . . .'

'Well, I'm changing my image, why can't you change yours? I bought a jacket and tie in a charity shop today, only cost me a quid. I'll be a changed man. I just hope no one notices my trousers . . .'

'Oh don't worry about them. All Tories have baggy trousers, I think it's because of all the keys they carry around in their pockets.' He puts some finishing touches to the hairstyle, then gives Chris the shaving-mirror so that he can inspect the results. 'Think you'll pass?

'Oh yes.' Chris squints at his reflection. 'That's very realistic.'

'How about a little grease?'

'Yes please.' Chris puts on his glasses and looks at the mirror again. 'Ah yes, you've done a great job. I look perfect. Now for God's sake take that mirror away before I hit myself!'

# *Unnatural acts*

The Marchant Building is set back a little way from the road. To reach it Chris has to cross a brightly-lit courtyard, and suddenly he feels like a prisoner trapped in the glare of a searchlight. Now now, calm down, he tells himself – you're hundreds of miles from home, no one can possibly recognise you. But he's still nervous as he enters the building and follows the signs to the room marked 'Conservative Party Meeting'.

Another bolt of shame shoots through him as he opens the door. Suddenly everyone turns round to look – and my God, that's Willy Preston standing over in the corner! And isn't that, er, whatsisname fiddling with the curtains? And that man who gave me such a strange look, I know, that's Martin Fisher's dad, though I've never seen him in a suit before, blue overalls was all he used to wear. And Chris feels for a moment as if he's stumbled on a meeting of some secret society, a Freemasons' Lodge maybe, because of all the accusing looks he's receiving from all over the room.

His composure is slightly restored when an immaculately dressed young man approaches him and says: 'Good evening, I'm afraid I don't know your face. Are you a new member, or were you hoping to join?'

'I'm already a member. I belong to the South Wales branch.'

'Ah, well done. So you obviously know Robert Flaxman.'

'Obviously.'

'Ah, well done. South Wales, how interesting. We always encourage, ah, intercourse between our branches. Tell me, as a

Welshman, what are your impressions of the big city? Fast, brash and slick, I expect.'

'Oh yes. Slick especially.'

'And our meeting – I'm sure you'll find it very different from what you're used to. But you'll find all our members very amenable. I mustn't stop you from, ah, circulating. And do help yourself to some wine. Now, if you'll excuse me . . .' And he goes off to greet a couple of elderly ladies who're hobbling into the room.

Chris takes a glass of red wine and sips it as he looks around the room. No, he decides, that's not Willy Preston standing over there, Willy's voice was never as fruity and penetrating. And that's not whatsisname, 'cos whatsisname didn't have that wart on his nose, and Martin Fisher's dad never did wear a suit, that man over there is a mere pale parody of him, a hollow laughingbox. Now Chris feels disappointed that there's no one here he knows – not even someone whose face he knows. All these faces are strangers to him, these smiles and gestures are a foreign language.

He holds his wine-glass in his left hand and then his right, he shuffles his feet and looks at the sagging knees of his trousers. Who can he possibly talk to? Certainly not that bloke, the one who's taking pot-shots at the ghosts of grouse with his invisible rifle. 'Bang! Got 'im. Bang! Winged the next one. Bang bang!' Not her either, the sparkling young debutante who's laughing like a polluted brook – 'Oh no, they prefer being on the dole you know, they're so much better off! Imogen used to go to the dole office in a taxi.' Two young men beside her simper in unison.

Chris notices that his glass is empty so he takes another one. He looks at the labels on the wine bottles, although they mean nothing to him. A limping man comes up to him and peers at the labels too.

'Oh, jolly good.' He drains a glass of red, then tries the white.

'Ah yes, jolly good.'

'Who'd be a Labour supporter? I hear they don't even serve wine at their meetings!'

'Jolly bad,' says Chris, trying to pick up some of the twang.

'I wonder which I prefer.' He smacks his lips together. 'Jolly good vintage. I think I'll have a glass of red first.'

Oh, why the fuss, they all make you pissed don't they? He looks at the limper's face, sees his strawberry-red nose and his porous spongy cheeks. Ha ha, there's no way an alcoholic can hide his addiction, pretend as he may that he's a connoisseur or caught the sun.

Not that Chris is one to preach about drinking. He's getting well oiled himself, what else is there to do? Someone hands him a photocopied sheet of paper, 'Conservative Party Activities – Spring'. A walk in the park, a violin recital, a trip to the theatre. Someone announces, 'I'm afraid there'll be a short speech, bear with us.' Chris's hopes rise and he clutches his glass with both hands.

A stout, hairy-faced woman in tweeds is struggling to extricate something from her pocket and slip it into her mouth. Chris is too tipsy and bored to worry about being discreet; he stares at her, fascinated, and the woman visibly starts when she catches his eye. 'They're just my vitamin pills,' she explains. 'It's the only way to stay healthy you know. I've almost given up eating food these days because it has absolutely no nutritional value.' Yes, and I bet you have a nuclear bunker in your back yard too, shelves crammed full of drugs and pills and a gun on the wall to keep out intruders. So this is the next stage of evolution, is it – Survival of the Fattest. Is that what they're planning in here? Survival of the Richest.

Two sharp handclaps bring the room to a buzzing quiet. 'Silence please! Our Chairman would like to welcome you to our meeting tonight.' (Hear hear!) 'Pray be silent for his address.'

Chris warms to this. This is the real stuff. He takes another glass of wine and prepares himself for a thumping-good speech. A bit of venom is what he wants, an attack on the layabouts and the wets and the Unions, and finally a rousing panegyric for the Victorian virtues of patriotism, self-reliance and cleanliness. But the speaker turns out to have a thin fluty voice and a large bald patch, and is no polemicist. More's the pity. Why, Chris thinks, I could do better myself, and me a mere rustic bog-trotter from the South Wales branch.

'I would like to thank Mr and Mrs James Habbard. Their vol-au-vent evening raised £40 . . . A picnic on Sunday . . . The greatest of all Bach's organ works.'

Chris glances around him to see if anyone else is interested in the address. Most of them are treating it as an opportunity to rest their jaws, grab some more wine or scratch their balls.

'And I'm pleased to notice a few strange faces in the audience.' Strange? Speak for yourself. Half the people in the room turn to stare at him. When he turns round they all look away at once.

He's helping himself to some more wine when a ripple of applause breaks out. The speaker bobs forward his head to reveal the whole of his bald patch, and Chris forgets about his wine momentarily as he examines it. It's glistening much more than when he started the speech, he must've been sweating a lot. Funny how smooth and shiny it is, not white and flaky like most people's scalps. Does a bald alcoholic have a red head? Chris is so preoccupied that he barely notices that the bald patch is approaching him, coming right up to him, and now emitting a sound –

'It's good to see some newcomers at our little meetings. Sometimes I'm afraid that we're becoming a bit cliquey.'

Cliquey, is that like clicking your heels? 'Ah, don't worry about that,' he says, turning his eyes sharply down to look at his face. 'Did you have a nice speech?'

'I see you're Welsh. We don't often get Welsh people at our meetings. Do you know Richard Hoover?'

'Oh yes. We went to a violin concerto together.'

The chairman takes a glass of wine and smacks his lips appreciatively. 'Are you on business in London? Or do you live here? Er . . . Mr . . . I'm sorry, I don't even know what you do for a living.'

Chris is feeling so light-headed that he adds a swagger to his voice and says: 'Lieutenant, actually. Lieutenant Evans of the Welsh Guards, here in the capital on leave from my regiment.'

Mr Chairman is hugely impressed. He raises his eyebrows and purses his lips. 'Indeed! Indeed! I thought I could detect the air of a military man! May I ask you, did you fight in the Falklands?'

'Yes, indeed. My regiment bore very heavy losses.'

'Well done. Well done indeed.' He starts nodding rapidly and rhythmically. 'Well I must say, it's a bit of an honour to have a war hero in our ranks . . . oh, ranks, no pun intended!'

'Ha ha.'

'A true fighter for freedom and democracy.'

'I most certainly am. But let me tell you, and I know all my lads would agree – it was Mrs Thatcher who was the greatest inspiration to us. It was her we fought for, you know. She was the lads' pin-up, the forces' sweetheart.'

'She's another Churchill, of course. What was it President Reagan called her – "The best man in England".'

'In fact, I was very much hoping to see her speak one day. So many times I've heard her voice over the radio . . . To see her in real life is one of my greatest ambitions.'

'Yes . . . yes . . . I've seen her in real life, of course, and I must say – but didn't you see her at the Victory Parade? Weren't you there?'

'Oh yes, I was there. But I was temporarily blinded by a gas attack near Goose Green. That's why I have to wear these glasses, my sight only came back a few months ago, and my eyes are still very weak.'

'Oh dear, that's dreadful. I suppose you're on long-term sick leave in that case.'

'Yes, that's right.' Chris repeats the words as if they're official military jargon. 'Long-Term Sick Leave.'

'So it's one of your ambitions to see her speak. I quite

understand that. My own happiest dream is to see her speak here, at my branch, and have me introduce her. But so far she's turned down all invitations. She's a very busy lady, of course. I hear she does her shopping at two in the morning.'

'Really?'

'But she does make frequent public appearances. I believe she's speaking in Richmond next week, one of my business partners will be attending. I'll put in a word for you, see if you can't go along too.' He lowers his voice. 'My business partner feels very, er, grateful to the brave boys who fought in the Falklands – especially, ah, the casualties.' Then he puts his hand in his pocket and says, 'This is my card. You must call me in a day or two. Now I must mingle, I'm afraid. It's been very nice talking to you, Lieutenant – a great honour.'

And Chris just stands erect and remains silent, as befits a military man. He glows with pride and with the wine, and imagines himself being described as a war hero and people looking at him admiringly across the room. It's time to get out of here, though. War heroes never hang around long enough to be chatted to. They might be found out. Besides, he's busting for a leak.

He knocks back the last of his wine and then slips out of the room. As he shuts the door behind him, his ears sigh with relief. He suddenly realises what a grating noise he's leaving behind – the screeching laughter and the clinking of glass and the general heartiness was really bashing his eardrums. Thank God that's all over. And he's got what he came for – he clutches the all-important card as he trots through the corridors looking for a Gents. When he can't find one, he goes outside and pisses against the wall. At least he's got a ready-made excuse if someone catches him *in flagrante delicto* – 'Well, if you're fighting, you're not fussy about where you go.' It's only natural, after all – though I bet some of those leeches in there would have me flogged if they saw this. That's 'cos they're so unnatural themselves, and proud of it too in their finery and twangs, proud to be so far removed from the animals and the great unwashed. Proud to indulge in unnatural acts like pill-popping and holding back a fart and laughing at an obscure Latin joke, and they cloak all their natural urges in ritual and mystery. What do they all do together? They get high.

But it's Chris who feels superior now as he makes his way to the station. *He* knows that only the poor and meek will inherit the Kingdom of Heaven. It's lucky really that the place will be quiet, not ringing with too much jolly celebration . . . Not that I want to consign all these people to Hell, oh no. It's just hard to imagine that these people actually have souls. I mean, most of them don't exactly seem to be the meditative type, except maybe the red-faced man in his cups . . . And most of them wouldn't let themselves be seen dead without the protection of their suits and ties.

Down the subway and into the station . . . He's searching for his money when a ragged little man with a weatherbeaten face tugs him gently by the elbow. 'Excuse me, sir,' he says through his grizzled beard, 'I couldn't trouble you for 20 pence.'

'Yes, of course,' says Chris – who can't spare 20 pence? He finds a pound note in his back pocket and gives it straight to the tramp without thinking. The beggar shambles away without a word, and it's only now that Chris realises that he's completely penniless. He could've spared 20 pence or even 40 pence, but he's managed to part with all he had.

His first instinct is to rush after the tramp and ask for some change. 'Excuse me, you couldn't spare 60 pence could you?' But begging from a beggar is about as low as raping a deaf-mute. Oh how stupid, how stupid can you get!

He scans the ground for an old discarded ticket which he could use – but the ticket collector is looking at him suspiciously, he won't get away with it now. He could go up to him brazenly and say, 'I'm a war hero, I'm afraid I've mislaid my credit card,' but the ticket collector would never fall for it. 'Pull the other one mate.'

There's nothing else for it – he'll have to walk home. Serves him right for being so pissed. And he heads off towards the street.

But halfway through the subway, he thinks again – couldn't he explain the whole situation, leave his name and address, and promise to pay later? He looks respectable enough with his new tie and haircut. He turns round, and trips over his feet in the process. He's scarcely regained his balance when a voice beside him says, 'Good evening, had a bit to drink tonight did you?'

His tone is so friendly and familiar that Chris wonders if this is someone he knows. But a quick glance at his face is all he needs – no, this is no friend of his, nor of anyone else probably. He's about 50, with a heavily-lined face and close-cropped grey hair. His haircut and jaw are very square. Chris stares at him in amazement for a few seconds before saying, 'Oh no, I'm not drunk.'

'No, I can see that. You been somewhere nice tonight? You're looking good.'

This guy must be either blind or crazy! Chris knows he's looking dreadful, with his ill-fitting clothes and straggly, greasy hair . . . Mind you, squareface obviously doesn't have much taste in haircuts. He starts walking towards the station, and says, 'I've been working late. I'm on my way home now.'

'Ah yes! And where is your home? Who do you live with?'

'Er – some friends. In north London.'

'So why were you heading out of the tube just a minute ago? Do you know where you're going? Or . . . maybe all that work has made you light-headed.'

Chris is taken aback. He looks squarely at his accuser and says, 'I lost my money, that's all. I wasn't sure what to do for a minute, but now I *am* sure.'

'So what're you going to do?'

'I'm going to give my name and address to the ticket-collector' – not to you, matey. 'I'll pay tomorrow.'

'No need for that,' says squarejaw. 'I know the ticket-collector, he's a good friend of mine. He'll let us both through for nothing.'

Well, that's crazy for a start! 'And what do I do at the other end?'

'Where are you going?'

'Kilburn.'

'Ah, just where I'm going myself. Come on, I'll see you're alright. You won't have to pay anything. No strrinks. No strrinks.'

You can't sneer at a free tube ride. Besides, it's wrong to mistrust a guy just because he's as ugly as a tower block and speaks with a foreign accent. So he follows him as he goes up to the barrier and winks at the ticket man. They both walk straight through.

'No strrinks.' Squarefeatures walks quickly and Chris has to trot to keep up with him. Down the escalator, sharp left and sharp right, hope he knows where he's going. A train arrives as they reach the platform, and Strrinks grabs Chris's arm and almost pulls him inside. Everyone in the compartment starts staring at them – oh shit, what do they know? What did the ticket man know? Who is this man? He looks for some clues behind that hard-lined face . . . I mean I don't mean to stare, but I've never seen a face quite like this before.

The train is leaving the second station before he realises they're going the wrong way. Hell, I should've guessed, this bloke's obviously a liar and mad as well. I've got to get out of here!

When the train stops again, Chris doesn't arise at once because he doesn't want Strrinks to rush after him. He waits until the doors are about to shut before he springs up and makes a dash for freedom. But he's too late. The doors slide shut and the train roars off into the tunnel.

'Sit down.'

Chris obeys meekly. He's feeling stupid, half-expecting to be told,'Why didn't you say we're going the wrong way, who d'you think I am and why are you afraid of me?' But instead Squareface says: 'You don't have to run away. If you didn't want to come home with me, you should've just said, straight out.'

'Well, you should've just asked, straight out.'

The man sighs. He produces his wallet and pulls out a pound note. 'There you are, there's your fare. Go on, go home.'

His face looks so dejected that Chris almost puts his arm around him to comfort him. But he thinks better of it, takes the money and stuffs it away.

'Go on, go home.'

'Well, thank you . . . I'm very grateful, you know.'

The man gives Chris a final imploring look and says, 'You couldn't . . .?

'I couldn't what? Give you some change?'

'No. You couldn't. Go on. No strrinks.'

# Wednesday

## Breakthrough

The first joint of the day normally makes Ratface go for a crap. But now he's been straining for about ten minutes without any luck – it just won't come. He wonders whether to give up, but he'll only be back in five minutes trying again.

What would he do if he had a job? Would he have to clock off and clock on every time he wanted a crap? He might lose a lot of money that way . . . Probably he'd become constipated if he couldn't even have a smoke. 'What do you mean, sir, a funny smell? I've just been taking my laxative.'

The door opens and Dan appears. 'Oops, sorry! I didn't hear you in here.'

'*Hear* me! What d'you expect to hear? Unlike you I don't fart like a foghorn to warn people off.'

Dan retreats and Ratface is left thinking. The secrecy's the pity. What a humiliation, to have to smoke like a guilty schoolboy behind the bike-shed! Why even keep it a secret from the boss? I should be prepared to take the consequences, if I believe in it so strongly. Martyrs have always suffered for their beliefs.

He starts fantasising about a typical day in a typical office: the phone ringing, making decisions, arranging conferences. There'd be all that gossip, of course, revolving around several 'key' figures – the boss, the boss's wife, the boss's mistress, the office creep, the secret boozer, hmm . . . the secret marijuana smoker. At least it'd be a chance to create a new stereotype, and maybe his reputation would spread quicker than if he stayed at home. Mega-corporation glory, from the post-room to the typing-pool! It's often said that the best way to change the system is from within.

Dan interrupts his daydream by shouting impatiently through the door – 'Hurry up, can't you, I'm busting for a leak!'

So he pulls the chain, although there's nothing to flush, and does up his trousers. He meets Dan by the door. 'I've been thinking,' he says.

Dan rushes in and relieves himself. 'Thinking? You're not meant to do that in the bathroom. What d'you think the kitchen's for?'

'I've been thinking. Maybe I'm restricting myself, staying at home all day, only meeting other unemployed people. Maybe I should go out and find a job.'

'Maybe you should read a newspaper first,' says Dan. 'There's four million of us trying to find a job already, and we can't find one!'

Ratface follows him into the kitchen. 'You see, there's a whole world I'm not aware of at the moment. The world of work. All these ordinary people who sit in offices all day and watch television all evening. Tory voters. *They're* the people I should be getting to.'

'Yeah, yeah. Why don't you start by telling your mother. Start by telling the police.'

'No, come on, I'm serious. I want to get a job, don't you believe me? Where should I look? What's this rag?'

'I think Patti left that yesterday. There's normally some jobs in the back.'

'Mm. Mm. How about this, then, this looks all right. "Assistant required for radical bookshop. Must be interested in radical issues, previous experience not essential." Yeah, that's perfect! I could really handle working in a bookshop.'

'So could lots of other people probably. When was the last time you had a job?'

'Ooh, not last year; I had one the year before last. It was mindblowingly dull, I had to add up these numbers all day long. I used to come home at the end of the day with nothing in my head but these bloody numbers. I'd be sitting trying to relax and my brain would be going "198", "3,141", "543", you know it was like someone had gone round numbering all my brain-cells – and I didn't have a lot left! And there was no one to talk to but this boring fart who was only interested in saying stuff like, "Ooh, did you know 242 is the square root of 12,192?", fuckin' L.'

'So what happened in the end?'

'In the end, well the boss came in one day and gave me this breat bollocking 'cos I'd copied down a number wrong. He was being really childish about it, I mean anyone can make a mistake! So I told him to eat shit. Fuckin' L, then he got really angry! Said he'd never heard such language, never! Never in his life! I think he was lying, but still. He gave me the sack.'

'So how come you reckon you could handle working in a bookshop?'

'It'd be different working in a bookshop, wouldn't it! I could read all day, for one. There'd be personal contact with members of the public, I could handle that. It's ideal, in fact, yeah! I'm going to give this guy a ring, you got five-pence for the phone?'

'Scrounger . . .'

'Ta. Haha! See you, then.'

It's a clear sunny day outside. Dan draws back the net curtain to examine the scene. A man and a woman are arguing; a couple of children are playing with stones. And – what the hell's this? I don't believe it, it's her, it's Margaret Thatcher, taking a stroll down Griggs Road!

No, It's not Mrs Thatcher, he decides as the woman comes closer. But she's got the same hairstyle, the same blue suit, the same expression . . . she's probably even got the same voice! God, it's like that woman outside the hardware store yesterday, looked exactly like the Queen with her headscarf and handbag.

And they go on about *us* wearing uniforms and imitating our idols!

He watches the Maggie-fan till she's out of sight, then finds a clean piece of paper and begins to write.

DEDICATED FOLLOWERS OF FASHION

About two years after the Movement started, the press cottoned on to us and ran a series of stupid articles about THE CULT OF HATE and FASHION OF FEAR. The dull hacks said we should be banned from the streets. Of course their articles had completely the opposite effect. All over the country, bored teenagers saw the photos in their dads' *Daily Rocket* and decided to join in. Suddenly the streets were full of phoney Creeps. At first anyone who even used the word 'Creep' gave himself away as a phoney. The press coined the word to describe and discredit the Movement they feared; but in the beginning we were just – ourselves.

Na was a Queen Di clone. She wore a Queen Di wig, a green padded waistcoat, Bermuda shorts and 'sensible' shoes. Molo's boots were the real shocker – made out of genuine animal skin, the ultimate in bad taste. But they'd belonged to his grandfather, and his image was straight out of a photo from that time, the Squire Riding to Hounds. All the pictures of the Squire Riding to Hounds show men with huge stomachs and glowing red faces, so Molo used to drink a lot to acquire the right sort of period feel. He was into atmosphere, Molo. There was nothing he liked better than standing on a street corner, bumming fivers, drinking sherry from a glass, and yelling 'Tally-ho!' at the frightened little videobook programmers who rushed by on the other side.

God, this is easy, isn't it! If I carried on like this for a hundred days or two, I'd have a book on my hands!

The press screamed that we were obscene. Maybe they were referring to me and my legs. In the early days I

> dressed like one of those old football players, with shorts revealing my bare legs. I strutted around, between the station and the telephone box, blowing a whistle. I wore a red shirt and my hair, permed into careful waves, sat in curls over my collar. Once a determined green-haired old lady grabbed these foppish curls and tried to clip them off with a pair of nail-scissors, but I gave her deaf-aid such a blast with my whistle that she leapt back and tottered down the street vibrating like a gong.
>
> But even I wasn't one of the real hard cases. The most feared, the most publicised members of the Movement were the girls who bleached their hair and lacquered it heavily above their heads. They wore dark blue suits and carried black handbags made from the skins of animals. The contents of these handbags interested the gutter-press immensely. Some suggested that they contained illegal copies of the 1979 Conservative Election Manifesto.

Dan folds away his writing quickly when he hears the door slam shut again. Ratface comes in shaking his fist triumphantly. 'Fuckin' A! Fuckin' A! I've got an interview, do you believe it, I've got an interview for this evening!'

'This evening! Good stuff.'

'It's a breakthrough! The bloke sounded really nice on the phone. I think this is my lucky day, hey make me a cup of tea will you, I may be a working man soon!'

'Yeah alright, you deserve it I suppose.'

'It's a breakthrough! Wahay! Hey, have you seen my skins anywhere? Ta. And can you lend us a fiver?'

# *Moral arbiters*

The psychopathic young men are gathered round the camping shop as usual, leering at the display of knives in the window. One of them turns and stares at Sue as she passes by. Fuck off, creep. God, I thought it was Tonio at first. In fact it looks like him, apart from that green tunic and he hasn't got such a smarmy expression. Ugh, anyway.

She really hates Tonio, she's decided. The way he was chatting her up last night, and then started on Patti as soon as she came round. Pathetic. Why do some men think you're available just because you don't have a boyfriend? He's a real boy's boy, the type of prick who really hates women – grovelling all over her because all he really wants to do is abuse her. Fuckin' L, who'd fall for that? Though some people obviously do, the way he carries on. Oh well, he'll get his reward in the end, herpes or AIDS – if he hasn't got them already.

And how Ratface can actually like him! God, Ratface would probably carry on the same way if he wasn't so stoned all the time. I'm going to have to watch him.

Faces look out at her from the dingy yellow gloom of the pub. A perfectly good day like this, and people can't think of anything better to do then sit in the dark and saturate themselves with poison! The busier ones, who can't waste time in the pub, are having to dose up on their poisons while they're on the move. Lighting up their cigarettes in the street. Puff, puff. Sorry, can't stop. Must go now.

Past the traffic lights and onto the main road, the street stinks like an airport. A van full of policemen stops for a young girl in a ra-ra skirt at the zebra crossing. All their heads turn to watch her legs as she crosses – will a sudden gust of wind enable them to do her for indecent exposure? No such luck, pigs.

It's a dodgy business wearing a ra-ra skirt. Sue would never dare, because most men are so stupid they think it's an open invitation, they think it means you're fair game. A-holes. What about Katey last year, she was standing at the bus-stop one day when this bloke walks by and sticks his hand up her skirt. Fucking Jesus. Some women would just feel completely humiliated if that happened to them – but luckily Katey's not the sort to take it lying down. She ran after the bloke, didn't she, sent him scurrying away, and then grabbed his ankles and sent him flying headlong into the council horse-trough. Good, put him right where he deserved, into a stagnant pool of green slime. Bet he had a lot of explaining to do when he got home to his wife.

The sound of singing reaches Sue's ears. In front of her, about a dozen immaculately dressed black men and women are singing hymns in front of a poster saying 'Jesus died for your sins'. Sue'd rather hear a one-man band or an impromptu jazz quartet, but since all that kind of thing's illegal, gospel music is better than nothing. Now . . . I need to go to the Post Office, I'll have a look at the bookshop, and I could use a little munchy too.

Sue goes into P. J. Morgan and Sons and finds the shop bustling with activity. Maybe they'll have a copy of *Sister Knowledge*, they've got a whole wall crammed full of magazines from top to bottom. She inspects the display, passing her eyes along the rows of hi-fi and yachting and computer magazines. God, does anyone actually read all this stuff, *Technology Now* and *Skateboard Enthusiast*? They've probably got a glossy monthly for cancer victims and people with lobotomies. Now here's the women's section – *Treasure*, *Woman's World* and *Modern Girl*. Vomit, eh, I don't want to buy a collection of cheesecake recipes and tampon ads, I don't care how shiny the paper is! Why isn't there a copy of *Sister Knowledge*?

Right next to the women's magazines are the men's magazines: *Brute*, *Knuckle* and *Cavalier*. A row of men, backs to the crowd, are flicking through the pages – Sue's not sure what they're looking for. Are they finding the best angles or the biggest tits or the most bondage, or are they just trying to imprint all the pictures on their memory so they can walk down the street with these hungry thighs in front of their eyes?

Anyway you won't see *me*, Sue thinks. She scans the shelves again, trying to find the magazine she wants. Isn't there even someone she can ask? But there's a long queue by the checkout, and all the other assistants are rushing to and fro. Excuse me! Excuse me!

The male assistant who eventually stops to answer her question looks at her as if she's some kind of freak. 'Oh no, you won't find *that* here! We only deal with the *established* publications.'

Oi, *Sister Knowledge* has been going for 15 years! But what's the use in arguing? The man's scribbling away in his little notebook, he's not even looking at her. Sod this for a laugh. Sue forgets about her craving for a Choc-o-nut bar and storms out of the shop.

Not an established publication, my arse! And they have the nerve to sell those obscene wank-rags . . . Oh well, that's different, isn't it, anything which degrades women is fine by us!

She carries on down the street, past the gospel singers, looking for another newsagent. Instead her eye is caught by a shop selling car accessories – alright, this'll do in the meantime. She goes in and buys a can of bright red spraypaint.

Clutching her handy-gun, half-concealed in its paper bag, she walks resolutely back to P. J. Morgan and Bastards. She'll teach them a thing or two. God, she's so angry she doesn't even mind if she's caught in the act – there are some things which simply must be said. What'll happen if someone rushes out and starts getting heavy with her? What'll she say? 'Well, you came quickly enough this time, didn't you!'

Now the psalm-chanting reaches a crescendo in her ears. She feels like she's in a film and this is the theme-tune. 'Without love, we are as nothing.' Ch-ch-ch! She shakes the aerosol vigorously in time to the music.

Better not spray all over the plate-glass shopfront. Sure, it's busy in the shop, but there's always a chance one of those dozyheads will see and stop her before she's able to write a word. So she finds a good spot on the brickwork, gives a final grand shake, then squeezes the nozzle and lets rip.

'This Shop Sells Pornography.' She lets the last five letters stray onto the glass, just so it's quite clear who she's referring to, then walks away still clasping the can in its brown-paper bag.

Her heart's thumping because she's convinced she must've been seen. She's expecting a policeman to leap out and grab her at any moment. As she pushes her way through the traffic of prams and trolleys, a black man steps out in front of her and fixes her with his eyes. Holy shit, what's going to happen now?

The man holds out a little black book and says: 'Have you heard the good news?'

Sue stares back at him in disbelief. He looks more like a hanging judge than a bringer of glad tidings. Now the singing breaks out again, mingled with the clanking of coins in a collecting-box. What's he going to say, 'The Lord will punish those who vandalise private property . . .'

Instead he says: 'Do you know Jesus Christ?'

'Well, not personally – I've heard of him.' She looks down at the Bible which he's brandishing. 'Your book's out of date you know. I'm more concerned with the present.' And then before he's got a chance to flick through his book and find a witty riposte, she dives off into the crowd. Come on, I've got no time for Christians! Especially not of the hellfire 'Burn Again' variety. They'd justify a nuclear holocaust by talking about Sodom and Gomorrah. 'Don't worry about earthly things', so they'd strip the world's resources and create a barren wasteland. 'Oh well, we've always got the next world.' Past a filling station – 'Thy name is Petrol and upon this rock I shall build my Church.' And how come this Lord's always got to be a man?

Approaching the Post Office, but – oh shit, I've spent all my money now, on that spraypaint. I might as well go to the park I suppose, rather than face P. J. Morgan's and the Turn-Agains again. Besides you can never be sure you're not being followed.

In the park she strolls around and then rests awhile, and feels proud that she's escaped to write graffiti another day. I can hardly believe that no one saw me do it! Did they all agree with me, or did they think I was writing 'Spring Sales' or 'Happy Easter'? Anyway, they *will* see my slogan. There'll be no hiding it behind a brown-paper cover. Young children will go in and out and ask their mothers 'What's that mean, mum?' and mum will umm and umm but won't be able to hide it 'cos it's out in the open now. And forever the name of Morgan's will be associated with obscenity, and mum won't be able to take her kids there again, and maybe the little girl will grow up with a decent sense of anger seething inside her.

Some specks of rain awake her from her daydreams. The sky has turned grey and a cold wind is starting to blow. Her feelings of pride have vanished as suddenly as the sun. As she walks back towards the high street, the skies open and pelt her with rain. She breaks into a run, and wonders if the downpour will wash away her words.

Past the garage and the accessory shop, trampling underfoot all the discarded paper bags and newspaper and sales leaflets. The streets are almost deserted now, apart from a few people sheltering under the awnings. Sue crosses the road to admire her artwork from a distance. It's still there, in all its scarlet glory, untouched and unsmeared. And now it seems to dominate the vista and yell out across the street. True, the hassled shoppers don't exactly seem to be discussing the issue in heated tones . . . But for sure that's what they're thinking, she thinks.

# *Direct inaction*

The balding man rocks back in his chair and says: 'I don't think we need go any further with the interview. Not if you haven't had any experience.'

Ratface can't believe that he's being dismissed so soon. 'But I read lots!' he pleads. 'Go on, try me! I know masses about books, I've got a really good memory too. I'd pick up all the technicalities in no time.'

The manager scribbles something in his notebook. 'Unfortunately we've had so many applicants. A lot of them have had several years' sales experience.'

So why didn't you tell me that when I rang up? Eh? 'Is that all, then? Don't I get a chance to show you how much I know?'

'It won't be necessary.' He's trying not to catch Ratface's eye – closing his notebook, putting it away in his drawer, rocking to and fro and looking at his watch. Ratface stares at him with a mixture of pity and anger, then stands up and leaves the room without another word. Well, you can stuff your bloody job, thank you very much! I wouldn't work in this tip, not if you paid me! I can see you don't have a clue about running a bookshop. I bet you just want to employ a pretty face, 'cos that's the only way you're ever going to entice anyone into this grotty hole!

There're still no customers in the shop, he notices, as he walks out of the front door. There was no one here when I came in either. Serves 'em right.

But – fucking Jesus! He curses out loud and stamps his feet. I should've told him yes, of course, I should've told a lie. You'll never get anywhere telling the truth. I should've said I had some experience.

His temper mounts, and he lights one of his ready-rolleds to calm him down. Ah that's better, much better. His brain lies down with a sigh of relief, but as the feeling of helplessness takes over he begins to panic. Oh no, I blew it! I blew it! Maybe I shouln't've been so abrupt with the silly fucker. But then, it wasn't me who started it, was it? He was the rude one, leading me on a wild goose chase. God, didn't even offer to pay my expenses!

He decides to save a bit of money by walking some of the way home. But the smell of frying, wafting from a fish-shop on the corner, tempts him to go and blow all his savings on a bag of chips. No, better wait till I've finished this spliff at least.

The sun has vanished and it's beginning to get dark as Ratface turns down a sidestreet in search of a short-cut. The houses here look like Victorian office-blocks, the home of many a harrassed clerk, I'm sure. They're quiet enough now though, barely a soul in sight.

He turns another corner, and runs his fingers along the metal railings which divide the backs of the buildings from the pavement. Suddenly he notices a man about 50 yards in front of him, looking shiftily around him before slipping through a gap in the fence.

Ratface carries on walking, and watches as the man goes from window to window, trying to find one which he can open.

As he gets closer, Ratty's first idea is to shout at the guy to scare him off. But he might turn heavy, pull out a knife or something – best not cause him to freak out and do anything rash. The best thing is to stay calm, stay quiet and play it cool. Now, what should you do in a situation like this? . . . Oh yes, call the police, that's what.

But – the police? The filth, the Old Bill? John Paul Watkins is no friend of the Old Bill. More likely I'm a friend of the burglar! I mean, it's stooping pretty low, one criminal grassing on another . . . And maybe he's not even a criminal! Maybe it's the owner of the place and he's just locked himself out. Or it's the night-watchman checking the locks are secure. Though, mind you, he looked like a burglar to me – soft shoes and bomber jacket. I wonder where he was hiding his swag-bag?

Concern for the culprit suddenly changes to concern for the victim. It's only fair to alert the police, tell them there's a burglar who's broken into a house on the corner of Milkman Street. No, Millman Street, after the Honourable Lord Millman of course. And Beston Road, if I can remember that. Now, there must be a Police Station near here. Ratface looks all around and can't understand why there isn't a Police Station or even a policeman anywhere in sight. There's always one when he doesn't want to see one, so where've they all gone now?

Serves them right if the bloke escapes, in that case. I suppose I should ring 999 . . . But then they'd only want me to make a great long statement about exactly what I saw, no, I couldn't handle that. I don't want to sit around in a dingy cell for hours while some pig says, 'Er, how d'you spell proceeding?'

I could give them an anonymous call . . . But they'd probably come screeching round in their cars and arrest *me* and charge me with the burglary! Shit, they'd find my stash too. Hee-vy! I suppose I look a *bit* respectable, at least, in Chris's jacket and Dan's jumper, but I don't feel comfy in them at all . . . They really don't fit me, and they'd probably charge me with theft of the jacket, too. 'Well, it's not yours, sonny, anyone can see that.'

Anyway there's not even a telephone box in this God-forsaken place. He walks on, still pondering the issue, but when at last he finds a kiosk, he knows it's too late. Good luck to the bloke, I suppose – who'm I to decide what's right and wrong?

Sue and Chris are playing chess when Dan comes in. 'God, you know the police have blocked off Smith Road all the way up the hill. I had to make a detour. It was some rabbi's funeral, there was a procession all the way up Smith Road.'

Sue just goes 'Mmm' and continues concentrating on the board.

'I thought it was pretty neat, though,' Dan goes on. 'I mean, I just did a U-turn and pissed off. But all these cars were stuck there! Ha ha! that's how I'd like to go, you know. Bring the traffic to a standstill.'

Sue says, 'Huh, when I'm dead, I don't want to be buried. You can just flush my remains down the bog if you like.'

'You crazy? That bog gets blocked if you put a fag-end down it!'

'Well anyway, I can do without some fucker of a male priest reciting a magic spell over me.'

Chris looks up abruptly and stares at her. 'Oh what?' Sue says. 'Is it my turn?'

'Oh no, just . . .' Chris moves quickly. 'There, it's your go now.'

Dan's reading Patti's magazine when Ratface comes in looking hot and flushed. 'Hey, didn't you see me back there Dan? You passed me straight by. I shouted at you, didn't you hear?'

'Oh, I heard someone shouting, I think. I thought it was just some pillock going to tell me my back wheel was going round.'

'How did your interview go, John?' Chris asks. 'Get the job then?'

'No. Fuckin' L. What a farce.' Ratface shakes his head and takes off his jacket and jumper. 'Wanted someone with experience, didn't they.'

'You should've said you had experience then,' says Sue. 'You give up too easily, that's your problem.'

'Oi! What was I meant to say, then? What when they asked me for references? Come on. I did my best, honestly. I really tried to sell myself – but they didn't give me a chance.'

'Mmm.'

'I bet you don't believe me. I bet you think I slouched in there and mumbled into my hand – "Far out man". Well I didn't. You should've seen how keen and eager I was.'

'Mmm.'

Dan breaks in – 'Hey, have you read this article about the transportation of nuclear waste through London? Fuckin' unbelievable.'

'Oh no. Is it good?'

'Good's not the word. You should read it.'

Ratface is rolling a little number. He says, to no one in particular, 'It was weird as I was walking home after the interview. I think I witnessed a break-in.'

'What d'you mean, you think? You can't just *think*, did you or didn't you?'

'Well, I don't know. It was down this deserted street, I saw this suspicious-looking bloke messing around with the windows. I think he got one of them open, I wasn't hanging around.'

'Sounds like a break-in to me! So what'd you do?'

'Well . . . what would you have done? I don't know . . . I didn't want to get tied up, know what I mean? Made to give a statement to the police, you know how slow they are . . . Anyway, I don't like to interfere, for all I know it could've been some bloke in need of a couple of bob breaking into the National Front headquarters.'

'Not very likely,' says Sue. 'So what'd you do, nothing I suppose? More likely it was some fascist raiding the CND offices. A right-wing arsonist, that's what the fascists are keen on isn't it, arson?'

Ratface sighs. 'I know . . . I know . . . But what was I meant to do, stop and ask the bloke a few questions? 'Scuse me guv, are your intentions good? Ho yuss, that's alright then!'

'No, 'course not. Should've done exactly what you'd do if you saw someone breaking into *your* house. Should've called the police.'

'Yeah, but that's the thing, isn't it?! I *couldn't* call the police if I saw someone breaking in here, not with all the plants we're growing! Same with tonight – I didn't want to get involved with the Old Bill, they could've busted me.'

Sue and Chris are engrossed in their game again. Dan says,

'Bloody hell, this is outrageous. All this radioactive waste just travels along the railway, completely unprotected, there could be an accident at any time. It says here an accident could kill millions of people.'

'I just – '

'And shit! Listen – 1/30,000,000 gramme of Ruthenium in the lung is sufficient to kill a person through cancer. There are six grammes of Ruthenium in one spent fuel container.'

'I know all that,' Ratface says. 'What are they doing, printing that? I read about that years ago. It's hardly new, is it?'

'It's fucking outrageous.' Dan goes on reading.

Ratface makes sure he's not going to be interrupted again, then says: 'But seriously, what *would* we do if there was a break-in here?'

'There's nothing to nick,' Sue replies, without looking up.

'But if someone called the police we'd be in deep shit!' He lights the joint. 'You know, I'm fed up with being on the wrong side of the law. I'm fed up with being paranoid, afraid of the cops and so on. I want to be a law-abiding citizen, I've decided. It's a strain being a criminal – it's making me old before my time.'

Sue's solution is simple. 'Then give up smoking dope.'

'I *can't* give up smoking dope! I mean, why should I? It's pleasurable, and I'm not hurting anyone . . . I want to smoke *and* be on the right side of the law.'

'Well you haven't got much choice then,' says Chris. 'You'll have to change the law, won't you.'

'Huh. Change the law. How?'

'Make a fuss. Create a bit of publicity, that's what changes things. You know what I'd do? I'd go and smoke a bit fat doobie in the House of Commons. Hit the headlines, make a national sensation. When all these issues are made public, well . . . good sense must prevail in the end.'

'We should be so lucky,' Sue snorts, turning down the joint.

Dan puffs at it cautiously. 'Look at this,' he says. 'If all the radioactive waste in one container was spilt, most of central

London would have to be evacuated for 200 years. Can you imagine, just a little railway accident is all that's needed to make London uninhabitable for 200 years.'

'They wouldn't even bother to tell us,' says Sue. 'They'd just let us all die, wouldn't they. Hey, Chris – it's your move.'

# Thursday

## *A blow against the State*

The early afternoon sun is beginning to shine through the kitchen window as Ratface re-positions his plants so they can soak up the rays. Ah, solar power – Ratface swears by it. Clean, cheap and reliable. Come on, my babies, drink up that sunshine! I want you to grow up big and strong.

He's so preoccupied that he doesn't even notice Sue come in. He gives a start of surprise when she says, 'Hey, that one's a bit scrawny isn't it? Shouldn't you prop it up or something?'

'Oh no, you mustn't help them. If it's too weak, I don't want it, I only want the healthy ones to survive.' After a pause he adds, 'You've got to be quite fascist about this.'

'Cuppa tea?'

'Oh yes please.' He starts to water the plants, and thinks – this may be the last time I do this. Who knows what will happen in the next few hours. This time tomorrow, my treasures may be famous – their names echoing all around the country, who knows, maybe all around the world. Mary-Jane and Gunter Grass and Non-Compost-Heepy, Beatrix Pot and Freda Weed and the Old Toke Tree. Be good, my petals. Don't fret if I'm gone a long time. What I'm going to do may help us all.

I just hope the police don't come and confiscate you all, destroy you in their ignorance. What a waste that would be. No, I hope that what I'm about to do will be the turning-point in all our fortunes.

Sue interrupts his flow of thought by saying, 'Can't you think about anything but your poxy plants?'

'I wasn't thinking about my plants,' Ratface retorts, sitting down. 'I was thinking about looking for work. Whether I can afford a newspaper today.'

'I'm going to the Job Centre when I've drunk this. Why don't you come along?'

'Oh – no thanks, I've got other things to do today. There's never any jobs at the Job Centre anyway, it's just really depressing.'

'Suit yourself. But there's never any jobs in the papers either. And at least the Job Centre's free.'

Ratface's gaze drifts back towards the window, and he has to check himself. 'D'you want a little smoke before you go, Sue?'

'No thanks.'

'I'll roll one for myself then – for later. I'm going out too, soon. I don't know when I'll be back.' So he starts to skin up. This may be the most famous joint ever rolled – more famous than the one the Beatles smoked in Buckingham Palace. Better make it a good one. Better make it look like a joint, to make extra-sure it gets noticed. Distinctively long and tapering towards the cardboard filter. Tight and white and twisted neatly at the end. What a perfectly smooth spliff this will be – a credit to the craft.

'D'you want your tea to get cold then?'

'Oh no, oops, I forgot about it.' He takes a few deep gulps. Almost ready now. Do I need a smoke before I go? Mm, maybe not. My judgement mustn't be impaired in any way – I must keep a clear head.

He puts the joint carefully in his shirt pocket. There, it doesn't even create a bulge. No one would even know it was there, my secret weapon, discreet and slimline so as not to spoil the hang of my clothes. Remember a box of matches, and now I'm ready for action.

Goodbye, plants. Goodbye, Bush Doctor and Puff the Magic Dragon.

Sue's putting on her shoes. Ratty's keen to leave the house before her, he always feels there's a stigma attached to being last up and last out. 'See you Sue,' he says, giving the bushes another glance. 'Good luck at the Job Centre.'

Goodbye, my dears.

Several times at the bus-stop, and several times on the bus, Ratface checks that his joint is still in his shirt pocket. Well, he might've inadvertently dragged it out the last time he checked. He might've poked a hole in his pocket. He knows he oughtn't to be nervous – but it's hard, when you're on the verge of making history.

He reaches Westminster in good time. Has a leak before crossing the road to the House of Commons, convinced that all the cops are looking at him. But he's got as much right to be here as anyone else. Well, not here, 'Members Only'. Er . . . Now, what's this, 'Stranglers' Gallery'? No, hang on, 'Strangers' Gallery' – that must be me.

He was expecting to have to join a long queue, but in fact there's no one waiting at all and he's able to walk straight in. Nor is he frisked, as he was expecting. Instead he's told to pass through a metal detector, and then he has to stand under another metal gate while lights flash and knobs click. An X-ray machine probably, Ratface thinks – dosing me up with more radiation!

'Right, you can go now,' says a policewoman. Several more police are standing around, but they don't seem to think Ratface looks at all suspicious. God, why not! He feels nervous, hot and sweaty. Can't everyone see he's an undesirable?

Walking through the lobby, which is lined on either side with statues of long-forgotten statesmen. There's a big enough paunch on that one, good grief! If he'd gone on a diet the nation would've saved a fortune on the marble.

At the far end of the lobby, people are standing around talking in groups. The gracious, gushing ones are obviously the MPs, the visitors are the ones who're trying to seem at home, and the young boys in suits are looking uncomfortable and don't know what to do with their hands, being too young to smoke or hold an umbrella or stroke themselves bald. A few more policemen are ambling around aimlessly. 'Strangers' Gallery?' one of them asks Ratface as he approaches.

'Yes please.'

'Take a form and fill out your name and address.' Ratface is shown into a little room to his left. He wonders for a moment or two whether he should give false ones, but decides that would render the whole exercise futile. Might as well be honest about it – say it loud and proud! Isn't that the whole purpose of this little plan, to get dope-smoking out of the closet, to rid ourselves of this soul-destroying secrecy and guilt?

So he writes, 'John Watkins, 74 Griggs Road, London', and hopes he's not signing away the life of his plants.

Yet another policeman takes the slip and says, 'Have you got any binoculars, camera, tape-recorder?'

'No, no.' Illegal drugs all right for you?

He walks along another corridor, up some more stairs and then another corridor. A sign announces that members of the public are forbidden to clap or make any disturbance or demonstration. What's there to clap about anyway?

A final check that he hasn't dropped his treasure along the way, and then he finds himself in the visitors' gallery overlooking the Hallowed Chamber. It's a good grandstand view, although there doesn't seem to be a lot of action down there. He takes a seat by the aisle and counts just seven members in the benches below him.

He looks around him. He can't see any 'No Smoking' signs, but there aren't any ashtrays either, and no fag-ends littering the floor. The Strangers' Gallery is full of tourists getting an eyeful of British democracy in action. When he looks back down at the Chamber, the Opposition MP has vanished – gone for a smoke maybe.

Today's debate turns out to be about the charity laws, and the speaker is managing to make it as tedious as possible. 'I beg to move, and I apologise for what might be considered by some to be a rather pettifogging and nitpicking preamble . . .'

Ratface feels like standing up and shouting, 'Get on with it, can't you, haven't you got more serious things to discuss?' But that's not what he came to the House to do. He's sure that Mr Speaker is staring at him, though he doesn't know why, except maybe because he's not wearing a tie and he's got a bit more hair than most of the people here. The Conservative MP drones on – 'The Charity Act of 1601 decreed that all goods, chattels, bonds, appurtenances movable and immovable, wards and plates, personal and impersonal, party interests and estates . . .' The sound of a long deep sigh comes over the loudspeaker system.

A few superannuated ushers are dotted around the gallery; They're wearing black suits and heavy gold pendants like glam-rock musicians used to wear in the early seventies. Ratty hasn't seen anyone wearing such an outrageous necklace since, oh, that Royal Jelly concert in '75. There were a lot of people smoking then, too . . .

It's a shame that there aren't more people here. He's fantasised about standing up in front of a crowded Chamber and casting the whole place into chaos and commotion. But at least there's half-a-dozen newspaper reporters in the gallery opposite; they'll make sure that the protest receives sufficient coverage. So, his heart beating fast and his hands shaking in the conviction that the eyes of the world are about to turn on him, he takes the joint from his pocket and lights the touch-paper.

He's still absorbing the smoke from the first puff when he feels a hand on his shoulder. He turns around with a start, and almost chokes. He exhales with an undignified splutter.

The usher says in a low voice, 'You can't smoke that in here, guv. You'll have to smoke that outside.'

Ratface blushes deeply. He tries to put it out with his fingers, but it the end he drops it on the floor and extinguishes it with his boot. 'I'm sorry . . . I'm sorry . . . I didn't see any No Smoking signs.'

'It said No Smoking as you came in. I should have you

thrown out for this. I just hope no one downstairs saw you.'

Ratface is about to apologise again, but the usher says 'Sssh!' and then retreats hastily. The Tory MP is still plodding away – 'I myself am on the board of many charitable institutions . . . My good friend, Sir John Haworth, is on the board of many charitable institutions . . .'

Ratface begins to wish that he *had* been thrown out. How's he going to make his exit now? What's he going to do? He leans forward and picks up his joint, which is now even more streamlined than before and bearing the imprint of his sole. Mustn't let it go to waste.

He cools down for a few more seconds. Sniffs his armpits – not too bad considering. Then he stands up and walks out, keeping his eyes to the ground. Away from the ushers' prying gaze. Runs down the stairs and, finding himself alone in the corridor, emits a yelp of excitement. He suddenly feels light-headed and jubilant to be free – it's like his last day at school, the last time he walked along those dingy, dusty, echoing corridors. Around the next corner he finds himself face to face with a policeman. Better look a bit dignified here – he slows down and assumes a serious expression, but inwardly he's laughing, mocking the policeman for his innocence. Down the main lobby, he feels bigger than everyone now. Hope he can hold back his laughter till he reaches the street.

Oh no – do I get another dose of radiation here? As he passes under the metal yoke, there's a click and his heart misses a beat then another spurt of panic – hell, they aren't waiting for me outside are they? Will they confront me, like a shoplifter, as soon as I try to leave?

But there's no one waiting for him on the street. No one's even looking at him. The traffic is still honking and roaring and the tourists are pointing and the flustered men in suits are still scurrying by.

A bus lurches past, crapping out a thick grey cloud of brainrot. Now, if I was an inventor – I'd investigate the possibilities of using marijuana as a fuel. Invent an engine which could run on hash oil. Then we'd be queuing up to breathe in the fumes! And everyone would walk around happy and relaxed, instead of brain-damaged and aggressive all the time. What's the problem?

# *The house seems very empty*

Ratty? . . . Danny? . . . Chris? . . . Hello?

Where is everyone, Sue wonders as she peers into the bathroom and into Ratty's bedroom to check that he's not lying in a stoned heap on his bed. She goes into the kitchen to make a cup of tea, and finds a note lying on the table.

'Dear Friends. I waited and waited with my brother Neil because I wanted to thank you and say goodbye, but no one came, so we had to leave. I'll write soon, hope you find work and don't let the Bastards grind you down. Love and best wishes, Your mate Chris.'

Sue has to read the note twice before it makes any sense. Chris never said anything about his brother coming for him. He never warned us that he might be leaving so suddenly. What's this, 'I'll write soon', isn't he ever going to come back? Where's he gone exactly?

And what's this card – 'Michael Morrison, Drainage Contractors, Bally Street W3'. What the hell's Chris interested in drainage contractors for? She draws back the net curtains in the vain hope that she'll catch Chris stepping into his brother's car. She wants to shout out at him, Come back! You can't just leave like that! But the street is deserted. She looks down at his bed under the table, and sees his jacket and tie lying there. God, he didn't even take all his stuff! Did he leave in a hurry or something? But it says here he waited and waited. It doesn't look like it.

Fancy running away like that in the middle of a chess game! Just because he knew I was going to beat him again . . .

Sue sits down and studies the board. At least he could've taken his move before he left . . . Now, I wonder where he would have gone?

She's still staring at the board ten minutes later when Ratface appears clutching a brown-paper bag.

'Oh, who else is here?' he says. 'You playing with Chris?'

She pushes the game away, and sends half the pieces rolling onto the floor. 'Look at this,' she says, showing him the scribbled note. 'Chris's gone. He just vanished.'

'Eh?' Ratface examines it and scratches his head vigorously. 'He never said anything about his brother coming to pick him up.'

'That's what I mean. Weird, isn't it. And look – he left his jacket and tie. Looks like he left in a real rush.'

Ratface peruses the note again. 'It doesn't sound like Chris, you know. He'd never've written "Your mate Chris", that's not Welsh, is it?'

'And it's funny, his brother coming down from the Midlands, I mean his brother works, doesn't he? And then going off again like that. Have they gone all the way back there?'

'You know what I reckon? I reckon someone came and took him away and made him write this note so's it wouldn't look suspicious.'

'Someone, like who?'

'The police maybe?'

'What, and leave all these plants here? Hardly.'

'Well, who knows? What if Chris is mixed up in things we don't know about. The underworld . . . He was always very secretive about what he did. He could've been taken away by a bunch of gangsters, you know . . .'

Sue gives a snort of contempt.

'Well, you got any better ideas?' He notices the card on the table, and picks it up. 'What's this, drainage contractors? You rung up someone about the drains?'

'No, why should I? I think Chris left that. It's strange.'

Ratface turns over the card and finds another scrawled

message – 'This man can get you to see Mrs Thatcher. I'm an officer in the Welsh Guards.'

'What, who's an officer in the Welsh Guards? Sue asks. 'This bloke Michael Morrison?'

'No, he's a drainage contractor. Chris is the army officer, apparently.'

'No. Bollocks. Ha ha! That little wimp, an army officer!'

'Oi. You never know. Though shit, I hope not – maybe he was a spy!' He lowers his voice, which was reaching a crescendo. 'I mean, you never know. Did he ever tell you about his past? He could've been anything.'

Sue shrugs. 'This drainage contractor can get you to see the Prime Minister, eh? That was one of his hare-brained schemes, wasn't it. He was really full of crackpot schemes, eh!'

Ratface was just about to tell Sue about today's episode in the House of Commons. Her dismissal of Chris's brainwave as a crackpot idea makes him think again. Was Chris just trying to get him arrested, or what? Suddenly it occurs to him how stupid he was to take such a risk, how lucky he was that no one noticed him despite everything.

'You been shopping today?' Sue asks. 'What's in that bag?'

'Oh, I just passed the greengrocer's. I thought we could have this tonight.' And from his brown-paper bag he produces a giant bouquet of broccoli. 'I got three pounds of it, it was on special.'

Sue groans. 'Fuckin' L . . .'

'What's that?' Ratface says sharply. 'Broccoli's good for you, isn't it? I thought you were a health-food freak.'

'Is that *all* you got? It's not very imaginative.'

'Well, come on . . . You should've seen the prices! Mushrooms, 35 pence a quarter. Courgettes a pound a pound. It's fucking outrageous. I could've got a few mouldy mushrooms instead, how would that've been?'

'I don't know . . . It's just, what're we going to have with it? The fridge is empty.'

'It can't be, Dan and Chris only went shopping on Monday.'

'Well, it is. Your friend Chris eats like a horse. Ate like a horse, I should say. We've got a couple of carrots . . . a few onions . . . a bit of rice . . .'

'Lucky I got this broccoli then, eh?' He rinses it under the tap and starts to chop it up roughly. 'I'm fucking starving. How about you?'

'I don't know. Depends on what you're making.'

'Whatever you want! Broccoli soup . . . Broccoli salad . . . Broccoli au gratin . . . Fried broccoli . . .' He opens the fridge. 'Bit sad, isn't it. We've got some jam, there's still an egg . . . I could make broccoli trifle.'

Sue's not concentrating any more. She's re-reading Chris's note. 'Don't bother me with trifles,' she says.

Slowing down towards the traffic lights, Dan almost gets a lapful of ash when a car-driver decides to empty his ashtray out of the window.

Than-kyou! Just what we all need, a neat little heap of butt-ends in the middle of the road. Silly goon. If any of them had hit Dan, he wouldn't've hesitated in pouring them straight back at him. As it is, he merely gives the driver a dirty look and taps his helmet before overtaking him. He draws up at the next set of red lights, alongside a shiny silver sports car.

After half a minute the lights turn amber, and for once Dan isn't the first to roar away. The sports car makes a sharp right, and goes straight into Dan's bike, which luckily is still stationary.

Dan glares at the driver, a grey-haired man in a pinstriped suit, and yells: 'You fucking arsehole, where d'you think you're going?'

'It's your own bloody fault,' the driver shouts back. 'Whizzing up suddenly on the outside like that.'

'Suddenly! Whaddaya mean, I've been sitting here for five bloody minutes!' The cars behind start tooting their horns, so Dan decides to put an end to the argument by kicking the car door with his left boot. But before he can make his escape, the driver flings his door open and almost knocks him to the ground. Simultaneously, a young skinhead, also wearing a pinstriped suit, emerges from the passenger side. The old man grabs one arm and the young one grabs the other, and together they tug at Dan, who's terrified that he's going to lose control of his bike and send it flying like a torpedo into the crowd which has gathered opposite.

'Kick my car, would you!' the greyhair raves. 'I'll call the fucking police, you little vandal!'

'Oi! It was you who went into my fucking bike!' Dan says. The tooting of car horns is becoming deafening. Sorry about this, mates! I hope these fellers will be finished soon.

Now a police car draws up at the lights opposite, and the two men stop their struggle. The older one raises his hand as if he's hailing a taxi. But as soon as the lights turn green again, Dan opens the throttle and roars off. He's not wasting any time talking to any bloody cop. Shame, he'd like to have done the bastards for reckless driving and assault; but he's too furious by this time, and he knows whose side the Old Bill would be bound to take.

As he approaches home, he slows down a little. At least he's sure by this time that no one's chasing him. He moves into the left-hand lane and relaxes – no sense in getting yourself killed when you're so close to home.

Suddenly without warning a parked car pulls away from the kerb and Dan has to swerve into the right-hand stream to miss it. 'Fucking Jesus!' He gives a blast on his horn as he draws level with the car. But the driver simply hoots back and shouts 'Piss off' before accelerating violently away.

Piss off!? He's got a nerve, hasn't he, after almost killing me! Fucking arsehole, hope he'll accelerate into the nearest lamp-post. Shouldn't be allowed to get away with it, the creep. Should I chase him maybe? No, what's the point, it'd only give him another chance to kill me. Some drivers enjoy knocking down motorcyclists, it's their sport. Well – I'm steering clear.

God, I hope Ratty's at home; I hope he's rolling a big fat doobie. I need a smoke badly before my temper explodes. Shit. I always need a smoke these days after getting off my bike. Sometimes I need one before getting on, too. Riding a bike – it's definitely a hazard to your health.

But Ratface is cooking when Dan enters the kitchen. '. . . Fucking drivers . . . Give me the shits.'

'Chris has gone,' Sue tells him. 'Look, he left a note.'

'That was nice of him.' He takes the message and reads it. 'Oh well, he said something about his brother who was going to help him. Not that I believed him, mind. What's for supper Ratty?'

'Well, I think it's strange,' Sue says decisively. 'Just leaving like that. And not even taking all his stuff – look, he left half his clothes.'

Dan looks at his jacket and tie, now hanging neatly on the chair.

'I reckon the note's a trick,' says Ratface. 'I think someone came and took him away and made him write this so's we wouldn't be suspicious.'

'Well, didn't work then did it!' Dan shakes his head. 'Come on, who d'you think Chris was? An international terrorist? Head of the Mafia?'

'According to Tonio,' Ratface says, 'he couldn't say what he did 'cos he'd signed the Official Secrets Act.'

'Tonio . . .'

'But according to this,' – Ratface hands him the card – 'he was an officer in the Welsh Guards. Look.'

'Drainage contractor? What? Oh no . . . Well, this is all bollocks, isn't it. This thing about Mrs Thatcher. I mean, he went to that Tory meeting, didn't he. He said he got chatting to some bloke who said he could arrange something. That's all this is – he was telling a few lies, that's all.'

'Well I don't know,' Rat says. 'It all seems very strange.'

'Don't worry about it! Easy come, easy go. Chris can look after himself.' There's a long silence. 'D'you think we should go ahead with this thing?' Dan says at last, picking up the card again. 'Chris had some funny ideas, didn't he.'

'Funny?'

'Well, pretty good actually. That one about smoking in the House of Commons! Ha ha! Take a bit of nerve, wouldn't it?'

'It'd take nerves of steel,' Ratface says proudly, 'as displayed by Yours Truly!'

'What, you going to try it?' Dan says with a chuckle.

'What d'you mean, going to? Where d'you think I've been all afternoon?'

'You serious? Naaa! Naaa!'

But Ratface's self-assured grin shows them that he's not lying. 'Honest,' he says. 'It sounded like a good idea, so I went ahead.'

'So how come you weren't arrested then?' Sue asks.

'Well . . . let's say – I didn't actually manage to finish the whole joint. Well, actually, I only took a few puffs. But it was obviously a joint, you saw me rolling it this afternoon Sue.'

'So what happened?'

'Well, this bloke in a penguin suit came and told me I couldn't smoke it in there. Said I had to smoke it outside.'

Dan gives a raucous laugh. 'Is that what he actually said! You have to smoke it outside?'

'Yeah . . . Did sound a bit like an order, in fact.'

'Well that's alright then! You have to smoke it outside! It's legal then, isn't it?'

'Yeah . . . I suppose so . . .'

'No more smoking and hiding, then. You can always just say, "Oh no, they told me in the House of Commons that I could smoke . . ." '

Ratface says: 'It's funny, really, after all the times I've sat here in this little room and shat myself that the Old Bill were going to come knocking on the door . . . And then when I go right up to the law and blow the smoke in their bloody faces, they just say, "Go away sonny, go and do it somewhere else". Where they can't see, you know.'

'Out of sight, out of mind.'

'Out of sight, out of *your* mind, you mean,' says Sue. 'Good, the evil weed is now the legal weed. You can stop worrying about it now then, can't you. Start worrying about something a bit more important.'

'You should take up Chris's other idea,' says Dan. 'About Mrs Thatcher . . .'

'What, pass myself off as a soldier or something? I don't know about that. I'd have to cut my hair for a start.' He chops some onions and lets the subject drop.

Dan says, 'If I was in power, you know what's the first thing I'd do? I'd ban all cars. Well, all private cars . . . I'd make 'em illegal. They're a bloody menace, they pollute and they kill – and all that lead poisoning, I'm sure it makes people violent. I mean, I'm not one to preach – '

'You do nothing else,' says Ratface.

'Eh?' Dan's taken aback. 'Whaddaya mean, I reckon I practise what I preach. Whaddaya mean?'

'Oh, nothing. But when it comes to being aggressive – I mean I've seen the way you ride, shouting and swearing and lashing-out at the other drivers. I mean it's not exactly mellow!'

'Well, come on! You've got to be aggressive on a bike, you've got to show these fuckwits you're not going to be pushed around. Otherwise they behave as if you don't exist. Shit, on the way home just now, a car went straight into me. Can you believe it, this car just drove straight into me! Sometimes I reckon they're all out to kill us, run us off the road. Hey, d'you know what time it is?'

'It's gone half-past seven.'

'Shit! I told Steve I'd meet him at eight. It's miles to his place, I'd better go.'

'What?' Ratface protests. 'You can't leave us to eat three pounds of broccoli by ourselves!'

'I certainly can. In fact that settles it. Shit, I thought it was about seven . . . Hey Sue, have you got any of that red spraypaint left? I'm passing under the Brentford flyover, I thought I might do a bit of sloganeering while I'm about it. Catch the attention of all the car-drivers on their way to work.'

'Yeah, good idea. It's so drab there, it can only brighten it up. Hang on.' She goes off and fetches the can, and Dan stuffs it down the front of his jacket.

'Well, have a nice meal,' he says picking up his helmet.

'Yeah. Say hi to Steve.'

A minute later they hear the roar of his bike starting up outside. 'I think he's in a bad mood tonight,' Sue says.

'It's not a good idea to drive when you're in a bad mood,' Ratface says. 'He should've had a spliff to calm him down. Damn, I wasn't thinking – I would've rolled him one.' Pause. 'You know, I've only had one joint today, the one I took to Westminster. Isn't that amazing! Better roll one now to compensate.'

So he skins one up. Sue says, 'You'd be better off cooking with that stuff, it doesn't damage your lungs that way . . . says me, puffing away . . .'

Ratface takes the meal out of the oven and dishes it out. 'Smells alright, doesn't it?' They eat until their taste-buds rebel and they can't stand any more.

'We can finish it off tomorrow,' says Sue. 'Good, I'm sure that was very nutritious.'

Now it's time for Ratface to roll his customary after-dinner smoke. Sue says, 'Come on, aren't you boxed enough?'

'Boxed enough? What d'you mean, I've only had two so far today. Anyway, this is a celebratory spliff – it's legal now, remember? There's no excuse for not smoking now.'

So they puff away and sit in silence for a long time. Was that a knock on the door? No, just someone walking around upstairs.

'I feel like going away this weekend,' Ratface says. 'Getting completely away from it all.'

'Where to?'

'I don't know. I don't mind much. I'd like a few days in the country somewhere, somewhere peaceful. I want to get out of this poxy city.'

'London always seems so grey when you come back to it, that's the trouble. So bloody drab and miserable and boring. It's always such a shock seeing it again, it doesn't really seem worth going away at all.'

'I don't know. You've got to take a break sometimes. Last time I got out of London was last summer.'

'How'd you go?'

'Might hitch. I like hitching, you meet unusual people. Yeah, that's what I might do.'

'Christ, you're lucky being a man. You can't be raped. I could never hitch, not on my own.'

'Yeah, only thing is most people don't like picking up scruffy young men. You know my mum, the only hitchhikers she ever picks up are soldiers and people in uniform.'

'Jesus! Soldiers! They're the last people I'd pick up.' Sue shakes her head. 'Professional murderers.'

'Still, I always get a lift in the end. Why don't you join me? We could hitch together.'

'Mm. No thanks. It's too cold to go hitching. It'll probably piss down all weekend.'

She starts flicking through the listings magazine, but her brain is swimming too much for her to concentrate. Her gaze keeps on being distracted by Chris's note. She liked Chris – it's a shame he's gone. She liked his optimism and his crazy ideas and his sense of humour. He was good company, Sue thinks – I'll miss him. I'll miss having someone to play chess with.

He was *ugly*, I must say that! And it's funny that he believed in God. But I'll say one thing about religious people – at least they don't treat you as a sex object, hassle or harrass you or try to chat you up. I always felt comfortable with Chris – what a relief that was.

Ratface is doodling on a scrap of paper. Sue says, 'I feel really tired suddenly. I'm going to my room to read.' But really she's feeling confused and lonely, and she'd rather be lonely on her own.

As she lies down on her bed, she can feel her heart beating fast. She's going to have to calm down a lot before she can get to sleep. As soon as she shuts her eyes her head starts swimming, caught in violent and uncontrollable tides. At first it's pleasurable but then her body starts swinging too, and her head's revolving so much that she thinks it's going to snap and she has to open her eyes and focus on the walls of the room to make sure she's still in one piece. God, this room's drab. Whoever thought of painting it brown in the first place? And I must get some new posters – I'm getting really sick of Ian Dury grinning down at me all the time. Doesn't he ever get miserable?

She turns over and takes a deep breath, and suddenly realises that her lungs have been starved of air. Breathe in, breathe out – concentrate, concentrate on breathing in and out – that's the secret, isn't it! She can feel her heartbeat slow down and the blood tingling in her veins.

Then she remembers her games teacher at school, telling her how to control her breathing when she was running. Breathe in through the nose, breathe out through the mouth. That seems to make sense – the nose is good for inhaling, it acts as a filter against all the bits of grot and groobly floating about in the air. So she starts to do what her teacher told her, and discovers that it really is very relaxing. Quite remarkable, in fact, much better than just breathing in and out through your nose. Really gets the circulation going. Must remember this, it's obviously important, makes your body function better. Makes you live longer.

But oxygen's important too. She must have oxygen. After a few minutes she summons up the energy to get up and open the window. Then she undresses and gets into bed. Maybe she'll do some reading in a minute. But first she must go on relaxing . . . She tries to imagine herself, very controlled, breathing correctly – walking down the street and breathing correctly!

Driving a car and breathing correctly! Talking to Dan and breathing correctly!

Now a monotonous buzzing-sound starts up. An insect has flown into the room and is flinging itself against the lightbulb. Maybe it gets a buzz doing that. Maybe it's just trying to kill itself.

Well, I wish it would hurry up, if it's going to kill itself. I can't concentrate, not with it droning and bashing away like that. At last she switches off the light, and the buzzing stops.

But now her teeth start hurting. I must make an appointment at the dentist tomorrow. I must, I must. Maybe I should write it down so I won't forget. And I must go on breathing correctly . . . Maybe I should write that down too, in case I forget. God, there's so many things to remember . . . And I've got that class with Patti tomorrow, and I still haven't found a job. The first thing I'll do in the morning is make a list. A list of all the things I have to do. I must, I must, I must . . .

# Friday

## First the bad news

Holy shit, I bet I've been asleep for ages.

She forces open her eyes and looks out of her bedroom window. All she can see is white. Oh my God, so it's happened at last! There's nothing, nothing there: the holocaust must've happened overnight.

A second later she comes to her senses and realises that the window is just misted over. She gets out of bed and wipes the glass. It's foggy outside, but she can see that the dull London skyline is unchanged – more's the pity.

It's nine o'clock, not so late after all, but Sue's wide awake now so she gets dressed and goes into the kitchen. She makes some porridge, just enough for herself because it's still too early to expect the others to be up. She's barely started eating when she hears some loud knocks at the front door. Who can it be at this time of the morning? The postman, maybe, with an exciting parcel? She rushes down the hallway, checks that her hair's not looking too ridiculous, and opens the door.

Her heart misses a beat when she sees two uniformed men standing there. Oh God no, it can't be the police, it must be the Salvation Army or something . . . But this time her first reaction was correct. There are two policemen standing in the doorway.

She feels like slamming the door in their face, saying 'I'm out' or 'I'm not dressed'. But then she thinks – I've got to play it cool. I mustn't give anything away. So she says, 'Yes? Hello?'

'Good morning,' says the first policeman. 'I believe this is the home of Mr Daniel Kinnell.'

Sue feels relieved. 'Yes, that's right. But he's not awake yet. You'll have to come back later.'

'I don't think you understand.' Both men take a step forward. 'We were round at your friend's parents' house earlier. They've already been informed.'

'What? Oh no . . . no . . .'

'Your friend was involved in a road accident last night. He crashed under the Brentford flyover.'

'Oh God! Oh God! what happened?'

'Well, the bike's well messed-up . . . And your friend, well, he's breathing.'

'Oh, God! He's not a vegetable? I couldn't stand it, a cabbage . . .'

'No, he's not going to be a vegetable. He's actually going to be alright, if the gods continue to smile on him . . . He should count himself lucky, because his helmet broke – smashed open like an egg, he might as well not have been wearing one.'

'So . . . he's okay . . . I mean – ' Sue doesn't want to ask too many questions, she doesn't want to draw these people in. Must you be going then, thanks for the news, well bye-bye. But the policemen come forward again.

'Mind if we come in? We would like to have a talk with you.'

'Oh no . . . if Dan's okay, we'll go to the hospital, can you leave us in peace for a while?'

'I said, mind if we come in?' Sue puts out her arm but the policemen push it aside. 'That wasn't a request,' the shorter one says as they march down the corridor.

Sue rushes after them – oh not the kitchen! We can talk in the corridor . . . But the officers seem to know where they're going. This'll teach Ratty to leave the kitchen table all of a mess. I'm not talking about my porridge, either. I'm talking about your bloody great bag of grass. That bloody great heap of roaches in the ashtray. A dozen little plants swaying blandly on the window-ledge. These creeps know what they're looking for all right. You might as well have put a sign about it on the door, eh Rat? A bloody neon light in the street. Sorry, Dan.

Ratface's dream turns unexpectedly bitter and frightening. No, that wasn't meant to happen, he'd've put an end to it ages ago if he'd known that was going to happen. He opens his eyes, hoping to be soothed by the daylight. But the voices continue. Goddammit, they're real voices! Shut up, will you? Goddammit, who's here and what's going on?

The voices are coming from the kitchen. He can't hear Sue and it doesn't sound like Dan, it doesn't sound like anyone he knows or wants to know. His first instinct is to try and go back to sleep and find a nicer dream. But the voices worry him – could it be burglars? He puts on his trousers and yesterday's shirt and goes to find out.

When he looks into the kitchen, he wants to go straight back to bed, nightmares or no nightmares. One policeman is standing by the window examining his plants. Another one, an ugly snub-nosed devil with a beard, is staring right at him. Sue's sitting at the table, her head in her hands.

He looks at the tabletop. Thank Christ, his stash isn't there, Sue must've hidden it! But his urge to smile is crushed when the bearded officer holds out his hand and says: 'Are you the owner of these dangerous substances?'

Dangerous? I don't have anything dangerous, constable. And hands off my stash, that's mine. Who invited you in here? 'You've got no right to do this. I want to see your search warrant. I bet you haven't got a search warrant.'

The policeman by the window says: 'We didn't need one. We didn't have to *search*, we just found this stuff. I've seen better hiding places in the police canteen.'

Sue looks up. 'It's worse than you think, pal. Dan's in hospital. He had a crash. Apparently – he's breathing.'

A patrol car is waiting to take Sue to the Police Station. There she's taken to a small cell and left on her own. To repent, confess or go crazy? She stares at the wall for what seems like hours, until colours and patterns appear and she feels she could swirl away and vanish into them if only she had the energy.

When the bearded policeman opens the door she carries on staring at the wall. She tells him her name and address, but after that she's not giving anything away. Her interrogator tries being impatient, he tries being patronising, he tries being rude.

'Were you aware that illegal drugs were being consumed on the premises?'

Oh shut up you ugly wanker, what d'you want from me?

'Who was the ringleader of all this? Did sums of money change hands?'

Think you're so clever, eh, foreskin-features, I wish you'd just fuck off.

'Do you inject yourself with needles? How much money do you spend a week on illegal drugs? Where does your money come from?'

Where does yours come from, dickface? At last she can't tolerate his stupidity any longer. She blurts, 'D'you have no compassion at all? Our friend's in hospital and all you want to do is get us into even deeper shit. What kind of person are you?'

The officer raps his pen on the table. 'D'you want to know why we came to your house to look around? Because we knew that your friend was a deviant.' Sue looks up. 'Here. D'you recognise this?' He produces a handwritten piece of paper from his pocket. Sue takes it and unfolds it. It's headed 'Dedicated Followers of Fashion'.

'Never seen it.'

'We found it in his pocket when we went to the hospital. It's the work of a warped mind.' He takes it back and folds it away carefully. 'And this. D'you know what this is?' From his other pocket he takes a small bent joint.

Sue shudders. Why the fuck was Dan carrying that? 'It's a cigarette.'

'You know very well what it is,' the policeman snaps. 'Don't play games with me.' Sue says nothing. 'You see, it's not our job to be compassionate. It's our job to clear up crime – to make the streets safe for ordinary law-abiding people. Working people. That's where our duty lies.'

Ratface is allowed to put on some underpants and socks and shoes, but the officer insists on watching him as he does so. Then he too is escorted to a patrol car, where he finds not Sue but a stony-faced man in a brown suit. All the way to the Police Station he stares at the road, he's expecting to see Dan or Dan's bike and be told 'Oh, that was just a trick to gain entry'. But he sees nothing of the sort, and no one speaks.

At the Station he's left on his own in a little room. At first he's angry, then he becomes frustrated, then frightened. The full horror of this morning's events begins to sink in. Oh shit, oh shit, I couldn't handle it in prison. And what's happened to Dan? He's not really hurt, is he? He's not badly hurt? It's a trick, isn't it, you bastards? I can't stand this. I can't stand not knowing. I want to get smashed. I want to get totally fucking obliterated.

The room is bare apart from two chairs and a table. The walls and door are solid. He can't find a spyhole, but he's still convinced that he's being watched. At one point he shouts out 'How about a cuppa tea then?' but gets no response. He sits down, he paces the room, he bangs on the door, he rests his head on the table, he lies on the floor. Still nothing. Jesus, I probably could smoke a spliff in here and they'd never know! But they've got my dope, the bastards, they're probably smoking it at this very moment . . . having a good time at my expense, typical . . . Oh I wish someone would come, and I need a leak, I can't hold out for ever. Are they plotting what to do with me? How to get rid of me? And where's Sue? And if those creeps *were* just lying about Dan, my god, I'll fucking kill them, I'll murder them for scaring me like this, there are some things you just don't joke about.

Oh Dan, Danny mate, you'd better be alright, oh I love you

Dan, you knew that didn't you, you've got no idea how worried I was . . .

He's about to start banging on the door again when it opens and another policeman appears. He sits down and produces a notebook and pen. 'I've come to take some details. It'll be better all round if you co-operate.' Ratface sits down opposite him and wonders when to unleash his fury. The new officer has a dark-red rash covering most of the left-hand side of his face, and Ratface can't help staring at it.

'Right then, what's your full name?'

'John Paul Watkins.'

'Address?'

'You know my address.' Pay attention can't you.

The officer refers to another page of his notebook. Then he looks at the earring in Ratface's left ear and says: 'Are you a sexual deviant?'

'What d'you mean? You serious?'

'Who was sleeping with the girl, then?'

'Oh God. No one was sleeping with her. Is that illegal? What's that got to do with it?'

'Are you a drug addict?'

Come on, this is crazy! What sort of a question is that? Still addressing the rash, he says, 'Look – what's a drug? What's an addict? Cannabis isn't addictive, d'you know that? Despite years of research, doctors haven't found anything wrong with it. But I'll tell you a few drugs which *are* addictive and harmful. Tobacco, for one. Work. Sex. Power.' (That's you, you bastard.) 'Money. Television. Sport's addictive – according to doctors, sport can be really bad for you. What about you? Haven't you got a drug? I mean . . . in a way, we're all drug addicts.'

The policeman stares blankly for a few seconds, then writes slowly, 'We're all drug addicts.' Ratface groans, and the officer continues – 'Did you know that you were growing illegal plants?'

'Look. I won't deny that I was growing them. But I ask you –

who was I harming? What's my crime? Haven't you got anything else to worry about? Mm? Look. Now I've got a question for you. What's happened to my friend? What's happened to Daniel Kinnell?'

'He came off his motorbike. He was badly concussed. A few broken bones. He got what was coming to him.'

What was coming to him? 'He's not crippled, is he? Oh God, is he conscious? Did you get the bastards who ran into him? Nail 'em, fucking nail 'em.'

'We won't be nailing anyone. No one except you lot. D'you wanna know, eh? Daniel Kinnell was probably stoned out of his brain on drugs when he crashed. What d'you say to that?'

'No . . . no . . . it's impossible . . . oh my God.'

'Eh? Eh? He was driving like a maniac. He was out of his brain. He was a good friend of yours, eh? It was probably *your* drugs which put him where he is now.'

Ratface clutches his head with his fists. Not the dope . . . don't blame the dope . . . Danny mate, I'll come and see you, and come and nurse you every day. I must hug him. I must say I love him. Tears begin to well up in his eyes.

'Crying's not going to help you,' Officer Rashface says. 'Should've thought about it before you did it, shouldn't you? Now, have you got anything more to say?'

'No, Christ no . . .'

He shuts his notebook. 'Thank you. I think you've said enough. We're charging you with the possession of controlled substances and growing illegal plants. We should be able to convict you nicely on this. Oh – you *and* your friends. Of course we'll be charging Kinnell too, as soon as he opens his eyes.'

# *Postscript*

Despite the predictions of scientists, the sun did shine that summer. Sue was convinced that this speeded up Dan's recovery – though it did take him a long time to get over the loss of his bike.

When the case came to trial, the accident wasn't even mentioned. Rat had always fantasised about making a splendidly persuasive speech about 'the freedom of the individual', filled with medical and historical references; but in the event he was too beaten and disheartened to say anything in his defence. Both he and Dan were fined £50 and bound over to keep the peace for a year. Their lawyer treated Sue as a halfwit who didn't really know what was going on, and she was let off with a £30 fine.

This put an end to most of their illegal activities, especially as they all developed a paranoia that they were being watched by the police and spied on by their neighbours. Ratface made the flat a marijuana-free zone, and only smoked at friends' houses. He entrusted his personal stashes to Harry and Nick and Tonio, so he still felt he was 'spreading the weed', but he cut down his own intake considerably. He bought a book which taught him how to draw by opening up the right-hand side of his brain. A couple of his drawings were printed in the new journal for the unemployed, *Free Times*.

Sue started giving Patti regular help on her market stall, and did a printing course at the Lavely Workshops. In May she got a full-time job at a radical feminist bookshop near King's

Cross, where she met some people who were interested in setting up a local women's newspaper.

Colin left England to look for work in Germany, so Di moved into Griggs Road. She insisted that the whole flat be redecorated and repainted in bright colours. She organised a party when Dan came home from hospital, with his leg and arm still in plaster.

Mick called round once or twice a week, and so did Lesley, and Steve. Harry visited regularly too. One night he appeared with a bottle of vodka and a litre of Yugoslavian sherry, to find everyone chatting with Dan's parents. Mr Kinnell pounced on the vodka and over the next three hours managed to drink almost as much as Harry. The others joined them and everyone got plastered. Mrs Kinnell spent twenty minutes trying to remember the tune of the new Police single – 'I'll be *wat*ching you . . . *I'll* be watching *you* . . . I'll *be* watching you . . .' Dan's dad announced that motorbikes were the only thing in the whole world he hated more than the Tory Party. Dan said, 'But in the right hands . . . I'm a good rider you know.' To which he replied, 'You can't ever get good at Russian roulette.'

Dan never conceded to anyone that he might've been to blame for the accident. He told his parents that it must've been a hit-and-run driver who made him crash. But he told everyone else a different story. He'd just finished writing a slogan under the Brentford flyover. He couldn't remember what he wrote; he couldn't remember anything till he woke up in hospital. But he was convinced that it was the police who ran into him.

'Sure, it all fits!' Ratface told him. 'You know what the police said when they were interrogating me? "He got what was coming to him", that's what they said. And they told me you were driving like a maniac – how did they know how you were driving?'

'I couldn't've been riding like a maniac. I hardly had time to get moving.' Some of their friends suggested that he should sue the police. 'Nail the bastards.' But what chance have you got?

Gradually their paranoias began to fade. But one remained with them, because none of them ever dared to voice it. It was – it was hard to say, because it was – that somehow Chris had been involved in the whole messy business. No one could think how, or why – but memories of him continued to haunt and mystify them. Ratface remembered the first words Chris had ever spoken to him – 'Did you expect a plain-clothes detective to sit down next to you?' And other things began to seem suspicious too. Chris definitely wasn't what he seemed – but could he really have been spying on them? Trying to get them all into deep shit? Could he have tipped off the police – and why, for God's sake, why?

Then one midsummer morning Di brings up the post. One of the letters is addressed in spidery handwriting to 'All at Flat 4' and she opens it with interest. The letter starts 'Dear Sue, John and Dan', so she passes it quickly to Ratface who's engrossed in his sketchbook.

'Hey! Hey!' Ratface springs up when he looks at the letter, then sits down again. 'I don't believe it. Did we ever tell you about Chris?'

'Chris? Chris who?'

He pushes away his pad and reads:

Dear Sue, John and Dan,

I hope you're well. I've been very busy. My brother found me a job.

I'm very well. So's my brother.

Bloody pain about the election eh, but never mind.

I've decided – first you should decide what you want to do, then you should do it. It's always worth a try. But remember, only a person with tunnel-vision can take in the whole picture at a glance.

Today the weather is beautiful. The sun is shining. But I'm sure it's shining brighter somewhere else.

How are you all. Please let me know. Why don't you all write me at the above address if you get the stamp.

Don't let the bastards grind you down.

Love and best wishes,

Christopher.

PS Too much smoking makes your nose itchy and wrecks your lungs.

PPS I got a job with British Rail. The boss is a Tory too.

PPPS Next week I'm being transferred. I'll be moving nuclear waste.

PPPPS I have some very interesting ideas about where to move it to. Stand by for action.